S0-CFG-022

# Praise for Murder Takes the Cake
# Book One in
# The Daphne Martin
# Cake Decorating Mysteries

"Murder Takes the Cake has all the earmarks of a good cozy: a mystery to solve, a cast of colorful characters, humor, and tiny hint of romance. It is a promising start to a new series. You did not think I could resist a one-eyed cat, did you?"
—*Literary Feline.com*

"Highly recommended. Five stars!"
—*Kaye's Penguin Posts*

"A very enjoyable cozy."
—*Vixen's Daily Reads*

"Murder Takes The Cake has all the right ingredients for a delicious read."
—*Ellen Crosby, author of The Bordeaux Betrayal*

"Entertaining."
—*A Bookworm's World*

"I can't wait to read the next one!"
—*Mystery Lovers Corner.com*

"Breezy fun."
—*Harriet Klausner, an Amazon Top Reviewer*

*ii*

# Dead Pan

by

# Gayle Trent

Bell Bridge Books

This is a work of fiction. Names, characters, places and incidents are either the products of the author's imagination or are used fictitiously. Any resemblance to actual persons (living or dead,) events or locations is entirely coincidental.

Bell Bridge Books
PO BOX 30921
Memphis, TN 38130
ISBN for Trade Paperback: 978-0-9841258-4-5

Bell Bridge Books is an Imprint of BelleBooks, Inc.

Copyright © 2009 by Gayle Trent

Printed and bound in the United States of America.

All rights reserved. No part of this book may be reproduced in any form or by any electronic or mechanical means, including information storage and retrieval systems, without permission in writing from the publisher, except by a reviewer, who may quote brief passages in a review.

We at BelleBooks enjoy hearing from readers. You can contact us at the address above or at BelleBooks@BelleBooks.com

Visit our websites – www.BelleBooks.com and www.BellBridgeBooks.com.

10 9 8 7 6 5 4 3 2

Cover design:      Debra Dixon
Interior design:   Hank Smith
Photo credits:     Cake/background - "© Gabriela Duran Fuentes |
                   Dreamstime.com"
                   Knife - © Gary Woodard | Fotolia.com

Recipes reprinted with permission from Holly Clegg's trim&TERRIFIC™ Gulf Coast Favorites cookbook and Holly Clegg's trim&TERRIFIC™ Freezer Friendly Meals.
www.hollyclegg.com

:Lj:01:

Dedication

For Tim, Lianna and Nicholas

Acknowledgements

I'd like to thank my wonderfully supportive and loving family. Without you guys, my life would be empty.

Thank you to my editor, Deborah Smith, whose patience and indulgence are greatly appreciated.

Thank you to Craig Gustafson, editor in chief of cake decorating's top magazines *Mailbox News* and *American Cake Decorating*. Not only does he support cake decorators though his fabulous magazines, he's a great guy. I had the privilege of meeting him at the 2009 Oklahoma Sugar Art Show where he chatted up decorators, wannabes (like me) and vendors alike.

A special thanks to Kerry Vincent (who makes a cameo in *Dead Pan*) for providing knowledge of the cake world and limitless encouragement. Kerry is the reigning queen of the cake world.

A special thanks also to Holly Clegg, author of the *trim&TERRIFIC*™ cookbooks. Holly is a fantastic cook who specializes in healthy alternative recipes for people who are watching their weight, cancer patients and diabetes sufferers. In short, Holly rocks! Visit her online at http://www.hollyclegg.com/.

Last, but not least, thank you for reading this book. I hope you will enjoy it.

# Chapter One

For the second time in as many months, I found myself telling a police officer, "I just brought the cake."

We were sitting in my cozy Brea Ridge, Virginia kitchen with its beige walls, white cabinets and light-colored wood floor. My kitchen is usually a peaceful, happy place. But then, I'm usually not being interrogated here . . . although, since I solved the murder of Yodel Watson, I am interrogated here more than you might think.

"Yes, Ms. Martin," the policeman was saying, "and the lab is already testing remnants of that cake to determine whether or not it's the cause of the death."

"Well, that's a relief. Or, at least, it will be when you see that the cake is innocent." It was also a relief to be dealing with Officer McAfee rather than Officer Hayden this time. Officer McAfee appeared to be on the backside of thirty and didn't seem to rush to judgment the way young Officer Hayden had.

"Nevertheless, ninety percent of the folks who attended the Brea Ridge Pharmaceutical Christmas party are violently ill today," Officer McAfee said.

"Right. As I said, I just brought the cake. I didn't stay for the festivities."

"Lucky you." His brown fingers fumbled with a small blue notebook. "You didn't notice anything unusual going on?"

"Like *Momba Womba* spiking the punch?" With a name like *Daphne*, I'm entitled to a Scooby Doo reference now and then, especially when I'm nervous. I can't remember what Momba Womba really did on the cartoon show, although I do remember he was a witch doctor. I'm fairly sure he didn't spike any punch, or else Shaggy and Scooby would've been in big trouble. Those guys would eat and drink things found in cobweb-covered cabinets in creepy haunted houses.

Officer McAfee's dark eyes widened as he leaned forward in my kitchen chair. "You saw somebody spike the punch?"

"No, no . . . I didn't see anything."

He stood up. "If you think of something—anything at all—that might've made those people sick, call me." He handed me his business card. "This is deadly serious, Ms. Martin. Fred Duncan is in the hospital in a coma today."

"Fred Duncan?"

"Yeah. You know him?"

"He works at the Save-A-Buck."

"Right."

I walked Officer McAfee to the door. "That's terrible. Do the doctors think he'll be okay?"

He shook his head. "It's not looking good."

I'd barely had time to absorb that upsetting information and put our coffee cups in the dishwasher before my neighbor Myra was at the door. Myra is a feisty widow with too much time on her hands, but she is always entertaining. I invited her in, and we went to sit in the living room. I felt I might as well be comfortable for my inquisition.

"Getting to be a habit? The police car, I mean. I thought I saw a police car over here." Myra kicked off her loafers and dropped into my pink and white checked club chair.

"You did. Oh my. You *did* see a putty tat. Or a police car."

She stared at me, unblinking. The Tweety Bird cartoon joke was lost on Myra. She was like a bloodhound with a scent to follow.

"What were they doing here?"

I sat down on the couch. "Brea Ridge Pharmaceuticals had their Christmas party last night."

"Were you there? Did it get rowdy? Was there a drunken brawl?"

"I delivered a cake, but I left before the party started."

"So you didn't get to see the brawl?"

"As far as I know, there was no brawl."

"Then why were the police here?"

"A lot of people who were at the party got sick."

"From your cake?"

I held up my hand. "Definitely *not* from my cake. Officer

McAfee said the lab is testing remnants of the cake, and I have no doubt it will be fine. No doubt whatsoever."

"Remnants? I thought only carpet came in remnants. Huh." She folded her legs up under her. "That Officer McAfee is a good looking man, ain't he? He reminds me of Malcolm Winters from *Y and R*. Of course, Malcolm is on that crime show now, so there you go."

"There you go," I echoed, as if her train of thought made one iota of sense.

"What was it that made everybody so sick?"

"They don't know yet. Fortunately, the company had some drugs on hand that lessened the symptoms for most of them. They couldn't help poor Fred Duncan, though."

"He still sick?"

I nodded slowly. "He's in a coma."

"Fred Duncan is in a coma?" She scoffed. "Bet he's fakin'."

"Myra, you can't fake a coma."

"Oh, honey, you *can*. I did it one time. Me and Carl had this big fight, and he stormed out. I wanted him to find me passed out on the bedroom floor when he got home so he'd feel really ashamed for how he'd left."

I merely stared at her with my mouth hanging open.

"I took a couple of sleeping pills and laid down on the floor," she continued. "I don't know how long I'd been asleep before Carl got home, but he was plenty worried when he finally got me revived. He called an ambulance and everything. And that wasn't like Carl. Normally, he was so cheap, he'd have just pitched me in the back of the Buick, turned on the four-way flashers and took me to the hospital himself." She smiled smugly. "Even with our insurance, that ambulance trip cost us a pretty penny. They checked my heart and everything."

"You didn't tell the doctor you took the sleeping pills?"

"Nah. That showed up in the blood work later. But by then, they'd gone over me with a fine tooth comb. I even got to have a CT scan. Let me tell you, Carl Jenkins never dared storm off and leave me again."

"I guess not."

"So, you see? You can fake a coma."

\*

Despite Myra's assertions to the contrary, I did not believe Fred Duncan was faking his coma. I felt horrible for him and his family. His grandfather and my uncle were hunting buddies, and I knew Fred's near-fatal car accident and resulting brain damage about a year ago had taken a considerable toll on the Duncans. Fred was having the worst luck.

My pre-teen niece and nephew were convinced Fred was "crushing on me big time" after he asked my sister a ton of questions about me at the grocery store and then ordered a cake for his grandfather. He'd ordered a birthday cake; and since Mr. Duncan's birthday was still months away, Fred's mother had called and canceled the order.

Pondering my recent past history with Fred, crime, murder cases, cake baking  and having to clear my name (not to mention the name of my cake-baking business) I decided to hop into my little red Mini Cooper and head to the Brea Ridge Community Hospital.

And I hate, hate, hate hospitals.

\*

I approached the two elderly women volunteering at the reception desk.

"I'm here to see Fred Duncan."

One of the women asked me my name.

"Daphne Martin," I replied politely.

Her eyes went wide. "You're the cake decorator who was accused of killing Yodel Watson with a spice cake!"

I stared at her. "My cake and I were cleared."

She tapped Fred's name into the computer before directing me to the ICU waiting area. The halls were lined with potted peace lilies. I spotted the door with the sign reading "Chapel" and considered going in to say a prayer for Fred. The chapel would be an excellent place to hide while I steeled myself to actually go and see him. On the other hand, if there was a grieving family in the chapel, that would be a terribly awkward situation . . . especially if it was Fred's family. I took a deep breath and went on to the ICU waiting room.

A nurse approached and quietly asked who I was there to see. I told her, and she led me back to a cramped room where Fred lay hooked up to a number of beeping, whirring, whooshing gadgets. A tired-looking woman wearing a pink sweatshirt and jeans sat in a straight-backed chair by the bed and held Fred's hand. I'd been standing in the room a full minute before she looked up.

"Hi," I said. "I'm Daphne Martin."

"The cake lady." She smiled wanly. "Now I can see why Fred ordered his papaw a birthday cake five months early. I'm Connie Duncan Fred's mom."

"It's nice to meet you, Mrs. Duncan. How's Fred?"

Connie looked at her son. "Not very well, Daphne. Would you talk to him . . . let him know you're here?"

"Of course." I moved closer to the bed. "Fred, hi, it's me, Daphne. You'd better hurry up and get well before the Save-A-Buck goes broke. You know they can't run that place without you." I looked from Fred's ashen face to Connie's.

"Thank you," she said softly.

"Can I get you anything? A cup of coffee or a soda, maybe?"

"Coffee would be nice. Would you walk down to the cafeteria with me?"

"Sure."

Connie went by the nurses' station to inform them she'd be back within five minutes, and then we headed for the cafeteria.

"I heard about the party," I said as we walked. "Actually, Officer McAfee of the police department stopped by and asked me about it. I told him I only delivered the cake and didn't know about all those people getting sick." I bit my bottom lip. "For the record, the lab is in the process of confirming there was nothing in the cake that caused the illness."

"I know, sweetie. This isn't your fault."

"What happened? How did all those people get sick?"

"I don't know. I only wish that if one of us had to be sick, it had been me instead of Fred. He's been through so much already."

"Do you work at Brea Ridge Pharmaceuticals?"

"Yes. I'm the bookkeeper."

"I simply can't understand how everybody—at least, everybody infected—got so sick so fast. Even if they contracted some sort of virus, it usually takes a few days to incubate, doesn't it?"

"You'd think," Connie said. "But the medicine Dr. Holloway gave out when people started getting sick appeared to help everybody, except Fred." She looked at me. "Why didn't it help Fred?"

"I wish I knew."

We'd arrived at the cafeteria. While Connie got her coffee, I stepped over to the soda machine to get a Diet Coke. I popped the tab on the can and took a drink. She rejoined me and we started walking back toward the ICU waiting area.

"I was impressed by how you found out who killed Yodel Watson," Connie said. "I read about it in the papers."

I grinned. "I wasn't all that impressive. I'm dating the guy who wrote the article, so he might've fudged a bit."

"No," she said, "I don't think so. I think you were very brave. You set your mind to finding out what happened to that old woman, and you did it. I admire you for that."

"Thank you." *Why do I have a huge knot of dread gathering in my stomach? Dread not even Diet Coke can wash away?*

She nodded and stirred her coffee. "I want you to do that for me, too."

I stopped walking. "Excuse me?"

She'd taken a couple steps ahead of me and had to turn around to face me. "That's what I want you to do for me. Find out what happened to Fred."

"The police are already investigating, and—"

"But you're Fred's friend. You *know* him."

*Not exactly.*

I started walking again, and she fell into step beside me.

"But I'm not a detective by any stretch of the imagination."

"Yes, you are! You solved that other crime and put a killer in jail."

*Yeah. I'm not looking forward to testifying in that case. Certainly don't want to get tangled up in another messy situation.*

"Mrs. Duncan, I'd love to help you . . . really, I would . . . but the police are doing everything they can. I'm sure they'll resolve this as quickly as possible."

When we entered the ICU waiting area, the nurse on duty rushed toward Connie and propelled her in the direction of Fred's room. Not knowing what else to do, I followed.

The nurse spoke in a hushed but urgent tone. "Fred is in some significant distress, Mrs. Duncan. We're doing everything we can do."

"Distress? What do you mean? What kind of distress? Will he be all right?"

If you've ever seen a soap opera or a movie-of-the-week, then you've heard *the beep.* As soon as I heard *the beep,* I closed my eyes.

*Please, no. This can't be happening.*

When I reopened my eyes, a nurse was pulling the curtain around Fred's bed and the doctor was approaching Connie.

"I'm sorry, Mrs. Duncan. We did all we could do."

Connie screamed, dropped her coffee, and threw herself into my arms. "They've killed him! They've killed my baby! You have to help me, Daphne."

"I will," I said, patting her back. *I have to. It's my fault you went for coffee.*

The nurses gathered around Connie. I heard one say they'd called her family. I waited with Connie in the hallway—mainly holding her hand, patting her shoulder and trying not to say anything stupid—until Walt Duncan, Fred's grandfather, arrived. I then excused myself and told Connie I'd call her later.

I walked down the hall and pressed the button for the elevator. I was relieved to see the elevator was empty. Being in a crowded hospital elevator is especially awkward. Before the door could close, I saw a tall, thin blonde woman with a briefcase and a travel mug briskly approaching.

I studied her while I was holding the "Open Door" button. "Cara? Cara Logan?"

She whisked a long strand of hair off her face with her wrist. "Daphne?" She smiled. "Hi! What're you doing here?"

"I was . . . visiting a friend. You?"

"Following a story. As always. My boyfriend works with Brea Ridge Pharmaceuticals. They had some sort of outbreak during a Christmas party, of all things."

"I, uh, heard."

"My boyfriend, John Holloway, saved just about everybody with some kind of miracle vaccine the company has been working on."

I merely nodded. *'Just about everybody' was right.*

"The only guy who didn't get better right away was named Fred . . . somebody."

"Duncan," I said.

"Yeah, that's it. Anyway, his reaction was more severe than everyone else's, and I intend to figure out why." She lifted her mug and took a drink of—given the scent—coffee. "I meant to talk to them upstairs, but they sent me away. Even threatened to call security." The elevator door opened. "Oh, well, see ya, Daphne. Maybe we can get together while I'm in town."

"Sure. That'd be great." I slowly walked out of the hospital.

Cara was a reporter from Richmond. How her paper had the resources to send her all over the place to follow stories was beyond me. Or maybe Cara was the one with the budget, and the paper just gave her free rein to pursue whatever stories she wanted to report on. Either way, it seemed a bit strange to me.

I'd met Cara a few months ago at the Oklahoma Sugar Art Show. As a cake decorator, I always pack my bags and attend. It's the Big Kahuna of national cake shows. Kerry Vincent runs it, and she's a star on the Food Network. On my kitchen wall I have a framed picture of me posing with her in front of a cake display. Anyhow, at the show Cara and I discovered we were from the same area of the country, and so we had lunch together. Cara talked in depth about her career. She flitted from story to story and subject to subject like a honeybee in a field of wildflowers. Buzz. . . . buzz. A murder in Kentucky. Buzz . . . buzz. Katrina restorations. Buzz . . . buzz. Fashion week in New York. Buzz . . . buzz. The Oklahoma Sugar Art Show. And now she was here in little Brea Ridge, covering a story involving her boyfriend, Dr. Holloway.

A story—given Fred's death—I wouldn't think Dr. Holloway would want told.

## Chapter Two

I got home, took a photo album from a drawer in the wardrobe that houses my television and sat down in my pink-and-white-checked club chair. My nerves were shot. When I'm upset, I calm myself by thinking about cakes. Fred's death, and then seeing Cara at the hospital, had freaked me out pretty badly. I tried to focus on my album from the Oklahoma Sugar Art Show. With any luck it would take my mind off Fred and Connie for a few minutes.

The detail on the cakes entered in the show's competitions had been amazing. Delicate butterflies . . . baby carriages . . . figures that looked as if they were made of porcelain. I'd taken photographs to show Lucas and Leslie, my nephew and niece. There was a character from the movie *Ice Age*, a cake depicting a scene from *Pirates of the Caribbean*, the cartoon character "Johnny Bravo," a Monopoly board complete with Chance and Community Chest cards, a dog with its toys, Yoda, Chinese food . . . and the darling, stand-alone sugar figurines. Entire sculptures made of sugar. Imagine.

And the wedding cakes! I haven't had many occasions to bake many wedding cakes yet—Daphne's Delectable Cakes is still a fledgling business, you know—and the only wedding cakes I've made so far have been practice cakes. But I'm hoping to add more wedding cakes to my portfolio soon. And the cakes displayed at the Oklahoma Sugar Arts Show provide such inspiration! The intricate scroll work, beading, gum paste flowers, lacework and paint. I really needed to brush up on my painting skills. Pun not intended.

One cake had love letters made of fondant with icing script. How many tedious hours went into *that*?

I turned an album page and there was a photograph of Craig Gustafson and Heather Walters of *American Cake Decorating* and *Mailbox News*. I had promised I'd send them something for the magazine; but I still hadn't done that. A girl gets a little nervous at the thought of sending a photograph of one of her cakes to the country's premiere cake-decorating magazines. Still, the chess board cake I'd made for Brea Ridge's Kellen Dobbs had turned out nice. I might send them a picture of that one.

Below the photograph of Craig and Heather, there was a picture of a cake someone had damaged. When I saw the beautiful cake with a piece of the bottom border lying to the side with the note *Spectator Damaged*, I had nearly cried for the decorator. To work that hard and then have some careless passerby ruin your cake and your chance of winning the competition was heartbreaking.

There was the photo of me with Kerry Vincent, the famous sugar artist, Food Network Challenge judge and Show Director of the Oklahoma Sugar Art Show. Chef Paul from Las Vegas had snapped the shot. As emcee for the onsite 'Divorce Cake Competition,' Chef Paul had regaled us with anecdotes—whether real or exaggerated—of his own unpleasant marital experiences.

I'd been a bit nervous about meeting Kerry Vincent. I'd seen her on television, and I was really intimidated by her. Tough but fair, she exuded a stern and pristine persona. This Hall of Fame sugar artist expected contestants to do their best work and really earn the honor of being the "best of the best" cake designer as well as recipient of the $10,000 prize money.

"Um . . . Mrs. Vincent?"

"Yes?"

"I'm Daphne Martin, a cake decorator from Virginia . . . and I just wanted to meet you and tell you how much I admire your work."

"Thank you. It's a pleasure to meet you, Daphne."

Her voice was Australian . . . not like the "shrimp on the Barbie" accents most often inaccurately associated with the country but sophisticated. Like Julie Andrews. I wondered if she could sing.

"Do you have a cake in the competition?" she asked. "If so, don't tell me which one."

"Oh, no. I . . . I'm here mainly to check out the trends . . . the new products . . ."

"You don't mean to tell me you came all the way from Virginia just to check out trends. Why on earth didn't you enter a cake?"

Man, nobody pulls anything over on *that* lady.

I took a deep breath. "I did bring a cake, but after I got here and saw the competition, I just chickened out."

"Daphne, shame on you! I've got a feeling you're in the habit of selling yourself short." She gave me her card. "Next year, I want to see you enter a cake. And if you think of backing out at the eleventh hour, you call me."

I smiled. "Okay."

She cocked her head. "What did you do with the cake you'd planned to enter?"

"I gave it to the hotel staff, and they promptly devoured it."

Mrs. Vincent laughed and hugged me. "You poor darling. You go home and gather up some self-confidence. Just remember with practice and dedication to the art you have chosen plus involvement in serious competition, your skills will improve tenfold. I'm expecting great things from you, Daphne Martin."

She was right about my needing self-confidence. My ex-husband's years of abuse had culminated in his firing a pistol at me. Fortunately, he'd missed. Unfortunately, his attempt on my life had netted him a mere seven-year prison sentence. That's why he's incarcerated in Tennessee, and I'm here in Virginia. When Violet, my sister, a Brea Ridge realtor, called and said she'd found the perfect house for me, I began packing as soon as I hung up the phone.

Looking at the photographs from the Oklahoma Sugar Art Show started me thinking I needed to work on my fondant figures in addition to my painting. I decided to start with the figure molding. My nerves needed the distraction.

I got up and headed for the kitchen.

*

I was getting ready to dig into a can of white chocolate fondant when the phone rang.

I plucked the cordless from its charging base. It was Violet, and she was speaking barely above a whisper.

"I need you to do me a favor," she said.

"What is it?" I whispered back. I don't know why I felt compelled to whisper, but it somehow seemed wrong not to.

"Jason's mom told me she got Lucas that guitar player video game for Christmas. I want you to rent a copy of it to make sure it's age appropriate."

"What's it rated? I can't imagine Grammy Armstrong getting Lucas a mature game."

"It's rated 'T for teen.'" She sighed. "I know he's been wanting one, and I'm sure he asked her to get it, but I'm hesitant."

"Well, he and Leslie are nearly twelve. It should be okay."

"Just check it out for me. Please."

"Okay. I'll go by the video store tomorrow."

"Thanks."

"By the way," I said, "Fred Duncan died."

"Oh. I'm so sorry." She was speaking in a normal tone now, so I felt I could do likewise.

"I am, too. Despite all the mood swings he had because of his brain injury, I think he was a good person."

"I do, too. I'll have to send Connie some flowers."

"You know Connie?"

"Not very well. I sold her sister-in-law a piece of property a few years ago, and I met Connie then."

"I met her today at the hospital." Later I'd ask myself why I'd felt compelled to blurt this out: "She wants me to help figure out what happened to Fred."

"Daphne, please don't do this again. You're a cake decorator, not Jessica Fletcher. Besides, it was 'Murder, She Wrote' not 'Murder, She Baked.' Let the police do their job, and stay out of it."

"I know, but Connie—"

"Connie is upset. She needs to understand you're not the

answer to her problem right now. And even if you do find out why all those other people got better and poor Fred died, it isn't going to bring him back."

"You're absolutely right, but—"

"Promise me you'll stay out of this. Be supportive, be a friend, but don't go playing detective."

"Who has time to be a detective, right? I'm too busy baking cakes, and soon I'll also be reviewing a guitar game."

Violet audibly blew a breath of relief into the phone and, thus, my ear. For a petite, bubbly blonde—I'm afraid I'm her polar opposite in terms of height, hair and bubbles—Violet can be a force to be reckoned with. Besides, she was right. I needed to spend my time baking, playing Lucas' game to see whether or not it was appropriate for him and Leslie and getting ready for Christmas. My tree stood in the corner of my living room —thanks to the help of my darling nephew and niece— glistening with its twinkling lights, red and white ornaments, popcorn strings and clusters of cinnamon sticks. It looked beautiful, it smelled good, but there wasn't a single wrapped present sitting beneath it.

She reinforced my decision. When I said goodnight and hung up, I had no intention of pursuing the mysterious death of Fred Duncan. I mean, the injuries he'd suffered in the car wreck that caused his frontal lobe damage could have contributed to his death. Maybe *that* was the one difference between Fred and everyone else who'd been infected and then given the vaccine. Case closed.

I really did have too much to do to play detective. And I really did have every intention *not* to play detective. And then my doorbell rang.

There was a cute, clean-cut young lady standing on my porch. She had long, straight brown hair, blue eyes, and she wore very little makeup. She had on forest green corduroy pants and a matching blazer. A pale pink shirt and taupe low-heeled pumps rounded out her outfit. She looked too young to drive; but there was a late-model sapphire VW Beetle with a cloth top sitting in my driveway, and I didn't see anyone else with the girl.

"Hi," I said. "How can I help you?" I was expecting her to ask me to buy something: cookies, magazine subscriptions, candy, raffle tickets. So what she said completely blew me away.

"I'm here to help you investigate the death of Fred Duncan."

Here I was getting ready to say, "I'll take two," when she hits me with that. I blinked. Twice. "Excuse me?"

"I'm Fran Duncan, Fred's cousin. My Aunt Connie told me you've agreed to look into Fred's death, and I want to help you."

I stepped back. "Um . . . would you like to come in?"

"Please." She wiped her feet on the mat before stepping into the house. "Should I take them off? My shoes, I mean."

"No, you're fine." I led her into the living room and motioned for her to have a seat. She chose the sofa, and I sat down in the club chair and tried to think of a way to explain to this girl that I'm not a detective.

"I read about you in the paper a couple of weeks ago," Fran said. "It was impressive how you single-handedly nabbed Yodel Watson's killer."

"I wouldn't say I did that single-handedly."

"I know you're afraid I'll get in your way, but Fred was more like a brother than a cousin to me."

"I understand, but—"

"And next year, I'm hoping to get into West Virginia University's forensics and biometrics program. I want to be a criminologist."

"That's terrific, Fran; it really is. But I'm not sure Fred's brain injury wasn't a contributing cause of death."

"Then that's the first thing we'll need to rule out. As a family member, I'll have access to information the hospital wouldn't give you." She got up. "I'm on it. As soon as I find out something, I'll be back."

With that, she was gone. And, just like that, I was smack dab in the middle of another investigation. Unless, of course, the hospital confirmed that Fred's brain damage had contributed to his death. Somehow, I doubted I would be that lucky.

*

I'd bought some molds at the Oklahoma Sugar Art Show. One was the figure of a woman. A recent issue of *American Cake Decorating* featured step-by-step instructions for creating a gum-paste girl holding a package to sit atop a cake.

I got out my materials—including the *American Cake Decorating* magazine open to the instructions—and arranged them on the island in the center of the kitchen. I spread out waxed paper, put my telephone headset on and donned decorator gloves.

I mixed some brown and yellow gel colors until I had a suitable blonde color. Then I used that color to tint about six ounces of gum paste—enough for two dolls' hair. I wrapped that gum paste in plastic wrap and put it aside.

I then used a bit of tan coloring to create a skin tone. I tinted quite a bit of gum paste this color. I knew I'd need extra if I botched painting the face. Those little eyebrows and eyelashes were going to be really tough to get right.

I tinted the remainder of the gum paste red and green. Even if I got frustrated and gave up on the doll, I could still use the green and red gum paste for decoration on Christmas cakes.

I took off the gloves and unwrapped the skin-colored gum paste. I tore off a small amount and rewrapped the gum paste. I rolled a piece of the gum paste into a ball and then flattened it out into a long, relatively thick strand. I placed this strand into the bottom half of the mold to create a leg. I repeated the process for the other leg. Then I placed the top on the mold and pressed the two halves together. I trimmed away the excess, and then opened the mold and took out the doll's legs. I bent the legs into a sitting position and placed them on a Styrofoam block.

Before I could get the doll's arms molded, the doorbell rang. *That was quick*, I thought, praying once again that the hospital had confirmed Fred's death to have been a fluke . . . the result of a preexisting condition.

"Come on in," I called. "The door's open."

But instead of Fran, it was Ben. Ben Jacobs. He's a reporter and editor for the *Brea Ridge Chronicle*, a freelance writer and a total HAG (Hot Available Guy). Ben has light brown hair that has a habit of falling over his pale blue eyes, a lanky build, and a lopsided smile.

We've known each other since we were kids and have been dating since I moved back here from Tennessee. He's never been married, so maybe he's not the type to commit . . . which is fine by me because I'm not looking for any sort of serious attachment right now either. Really. I'm not.

"It's not like you to leave your door unlocked and invite visitors in sight unseen," Ben said. "You must be expecting someone."

"I'm afraid I am."

He looked so handsome and so comfortable leaning there against the doorpost. He was wearing khaki pants and a light blue denim shirt that brought out his eyes. He made himself right at home when he was here. I wondered if he was at ease like that everywhere or if it had something to do with me. Maybe I made him feel at home.

He arched a brow, which nearly hid beneath that strand of wavy hair that had fallen into his eyes. If I wasn't working with gum paste, I'd brush it away.

"So who's this scary visitor?" he asked.

I smiled. "She's not scary. What scares me about her is that she's a Nancy Drew wannabe, and she wants to help me investigate Fred Duncan's death. Fred's her cousin."

"Since when are you investigating Fred Duncan's death?"

I explained to him how I was there with Connie when Fred died and how she'd asked me to help her. Then I relayed my conversation with Violet and my visit with Fran.

"So you're thinking Fran will come back here, tell you Fred's year-old brain injury contributed to his death and that will be the end of it."

I grimaced and bobbed my head from side to side. "Hoping, I think, would be a better word. Really, really hoping. What? You don't think so?"

"I don't know, Daphne. The entire situation seems suspect to me. Two-thirds of the guests at a Christmas party suddenly fall ill?"

"It wasn't the cake," I said quickly. "The police are almost sure of that. You see, not everyone who got sick *ate* the cake, so it had to have been something else."

"Which is good. But it had to be something."

"Don't tell me you believe this was all an elaborate plot to kill poor Fred."

"No. I think Fred wound up in the wrong place at the wrong time. But there's a reason that many people got sick that fast."

My shoulders slumped. "And we need to find out what that reason is."

*

Ben had left, and I'd finished the gum paste dolls. They actually looked pretty good. Leaving the dolls sitting on Styrofoam blocks on the island to set, I slipped on my jacket and took a piece of ham out of the refrigerator. Then I went onto the porch and called for Sparrow.

Sparrow, it seems, came with the house. Not long after I moved here, I caught a fleeting glimpse of the skinny little one-eyed Persian and began to feed her. She isn't skinny anymore, but she still is a bit skittish. Lucas and Leslie named her Sparrow in honor of Johnny Depp's character, Captain Jack Sparrow. They said the one eye made her look like a pirate cat.

I saw the cat emerge slowly from beneath a bush at the upper end of my backyard.

"Come on, Sparrow." I tore off a piece of the ham and tossed it just beyond the porch.

She hurried to get it, watching to be sure I didn't make any sudden movements. As she ate, I tossed another piece of ham—this one, a little closer to where I sat. She came and ate that one, too.

We've been practicing this exercise for a few weeks now, and it's beginning to pay off. I can't actually pet Sparrow yet, but she will brush up against me occasionally now.

I kept throwing bits of ham until Sparrow was coming within a foot of me. I decided to try something new with the last piece. I held it out toward her. She took a step forward and extended her neck so she could sniff the ham. She looked at me expectantly, waiting for me to drop it. I continued to hold the morsel out to her.

"Come on, girl," I said softly. "You can have it."

Her expression seemed to say, "If I can have it, then drop it."

Reluctantly, I did drop it in front of her. She ate it, but she didn't hurry away as I'd expected. I stood and, although she darted out of reach, she didn't flee the porch. We were making progress.

I stepped back inside and retrieved the bag of cat food I'd bought at Dobbs Pet Store. As I filled Sparrow's bowl, she brushed against the back of my leg. She then moved to what she apparently considered a safe distance away until I returned to the house. Then, she came to the bowl and ate. She looked up once to see me standing at the window, stared at me for a moment, and then continued eating her meal. I smiled to myself. Yes, we were definitely making progress.

Fran's little blue Beetle pulled into the driveway. I was still hoping for good news; but even if the hospital and Fran were convinced Fred's death was at least partially due to his preexisting condition, Ben wasn't. On the other hand, Ben wasn't actually expecting me to investigate . . . was he?

I opened the door. "Hi, Fran. Any news?"

From the corner of my eye, I saw Sparrow sprint around the side of the house.

"Cute cat," Fran said. "I'm sorry I scared her."

"That's okay. She'll be back once we go inside." I held open the door, and Fran preceded me into the living room.

"Sorry it took me so long. I had to convince the hospital I truly am a relative and not just some nosy kid or a reporter or something. They've apparently been having trouble with reporters trying to gather information. And, naturally, they have to tell these people, 'Hello? We're running a hospital, not a news bureau.' Anyway, the hospital finally revealed that they don't believe Fred's death was due to his brain injury." She pushed a strand of hair behind her ear. "In fact, they're as perplexed as we are as to why everyone else got better and Fred didn't. But they won't know more until they get the autopsy results."

I nodded, silently taking all this in and waiting for the other shoe to drop.

"What do we do next?" Fran asked.

*There it went.*

\*

I told Fran I had some cakes to finish up and that I did my best thinking while I worked. We went into the kitchen, where Fran immediately noticed the gum paste figurines.

"What pretty little dolls!"

"Thank you," I said. "They're made of gum paste."

"You made these? Wow."

"Painting the faces was the hardest part. Doing such tiny detail work makes me nervous."

"I can imagine. What is gum paste anyway?"

"It's a sugar dough." I grinned. "Kind of like Play Dough, but you can eat it."

"Kids in my elementary school wouldn't have known the difference. One kid was always nibbling his modeling clay. Now he's our high school's first string quarterback. Go figure."

I laughed. "Is he a HAG—Hot Available Guy?"

"Um . . . he's hot, I guess. But I think he's dating one of the cheerleaders. Not that I care. He's totally not my type. I mean, I'm not even sure I have a type; but if ditzy girls in short skirts are his type, then I'm not it, so he must not be my type either. Right?"

I gave her a slight nod and wasn't all that clear on what she'd said. Either way, I thought she was being a little too emphatic about not liking this guy, but I kept my opinion to myself.

I took four, one-quarter, sheet cakes from the refrigerator. "While these are warming to room temperature, I'm going to start preparing the decorations."

"Who are they for?" Fran asked.

"Since the Save-A-Buck doesn't have a bakery staff, Mr. Franklin has me make cakes for them to sell. He specifically requested birthday cakes this week. I'm making two for girls and two for boys."

"Cool."

"Want to learn how to make a butter cream rose?" I asked.

"Sure."

I jerked my head toward the wall pegs that held my aprons. "Grab yourself an apron and wash your hands. I'll show you a super-easy trick."

When Fran was ready, I handed her a flower nail and a bag of dark pink icing with a Number One-Zero-Four rose tip. I had the same tools. I took a red gumdrop and secured it to my flower nail with a dab of icing.

"Normally, I would use icing with a Number Twelve round tip to make a cone-shaped base for the rose. But since this is for a little girl's cake, I'm using gumdrops. I got the idea from a cake decorators' discussion group." I smiled. "Didn't you always want one of the biggest roses on your slice of birthday cake? This way, when the birthday girl bites into that rose, she'll get another sweet surprise."

Fran giggled. "That is totally cool!" She placed a gumdrop onto her flower nail. "Now what?"

"Okay. Let's start at the top and make the inner petal. Then, slowly spinning the flower nail, we'll add three rows of petals."

Her first effort wasn't too bad, but she wasn't satisfied.

"I have an idea." I took a six-inch round cake from the refrigerator. "When my niece and nephew visit, we make what we call 'bitty cakes' because they're small. Why don't you keep practicing your roses; and before you leave, we'll use them to decorate this bitty cake for you to take home."

"That sounds great. Thank you."

We continued to work on our roses.

"The hospital doesn't think Fred's prior brain injury had any bearing on this incident, right?" I asked.

"Um . . . they don't think it contributed to his death, if that's what you're saying."

"That's what I'm saying. I'm sorry. It's kind of difficult for me to discuss Fred's death with you."

"It's okay," Fran said. "I'm mature enough to handle this. Plus, I know that now is not the time to grieve. Now is the time—while the evidence is still readily available—to determine what happened to my cousin."

"Gee," I said, "you *are* mature. But you don't have to be Supergirl, you know."

"I know."

"Once again, we know Fred's brain injury didn't play a part in his death; but *something* did. There was something different about Fred . . . something none of the other victims had. That's why they recovered, and he didn't."

"We need to find out what that something was," Fran said. "But where do we start?"

"How about we start by talking to your Aunt Connie? Do you think she'd be up to having breakfast tomorrow morning?"

"I'll check with her and see. Where would you like to meet for breakfast?"

"How about here?"

\*

"Hi, Ned. It's me, Nancy," I said when Ben answered his phone.

He chuckled. "Did you hear back from the junior detective?"

"I did. Actually, that's why I'm calling. She's bringing her Aunt Connie—Fred's mother—to breakfast here tomorrow morning. Would you like to join us?"

"Are you kidding? I'll jump at any excuse to have you prepare me a meal."

*Mental note: invite Ben for more home-cooked meals.* "The

hospital records didn't implicate Fred's prior brain injury in his death."

"I figured as much," he said. "I'd love to sneak a peek at that autopsy report when it's available."

"I'd love to snoop around Fred's room. Maybe he was on drugs or something."

"I guess we'll find that out soon enough. Any drug would show up on a tox screen."

After talking with Ben, I decided to go to the supermarket to drop off the birthday cakes and to get some ingredients for dishes I'd be making tomorrow morning. Prior to my trip to the Save-A-Buck, I went by the Brea Ridge Rental Center and got the game system and game Violet wanted me to check out. At least, that was one investigation I could be up front with her about.

I'd expected a solemn staff at the Save-A-Buck; and for the most part, I was right. The baggers and cashiers were subdued, and Juanita's nearly nonexistent mascara indicated she'd been crying. Mr. Franklin, however, was a different story.

"Good evening, Ms. Martin," he said, hurrying from the middle of the store to inspect the cakes I'd brought. "Oh, these look beautiful! They'll be gone in no time."

"I have two more in the car," I said. "I'll get them and be right back. By the way, I'm so sorry about Fred."

"Oh, yes, so are we. What a tragedy, huh? Do you need help with those cakes?"

"No . . . I can get them."

"Great. I'll get you a receipt." He was whistling as he walked toward his office.

I went back out to my car and retrieved the other two cakes. I took them inside and placed them on the small display table with the other two. I then got a buggy and began doing my shopping.

I was in the juice aisle when I felt someone's presence by my left elbow. I turned to see China York, blue eyes sparkling, iron gray braids hanging to her waist. As usual, she was wearing jeans and a man's flannel shirt over a white tee shirt.

I smiled broadly. "China, how wonderful to see you."

"You, too. Heard about Fred. You lookin' in to it?"

I glanced around. "Unofficially. Why? Do you know something?"

"I know Fred went over to Haysi a lot. My cousin's youngest girl works in a gas station over there . . . said he came in real regular."

I frowned. "What's in Haysi?"

"You tell me." She patted my arm. "I'll let you know if I hear anything else."

"Thanks, China."

I finished my shopping and went through Juanita's line. She's my favorite cashier. I'll usually go through her line even if there's a wait.

"How are you?" I asked.

"Me? I am good. But, also, I am sad."

"I am, too. Poor Fred . . . and his family."

"Yes," she said, her eyes welling. "To suffer such a loss at this special time of year. It will never be the same for his mother. Christmas will now always be tinged with sadness for her."

Mr. Franklin walked over and handed me the receipt for the cakes. Then he looked sharply at Juanita. "Ms. Ramirez, do you need a break?"

"No, Mr. Franklin. I am fine." She quickly began scanning my items.

Mr. Franklin smiled at me. "Did you find everything okay?"

I nodded. "Just fine."

"Let me get a bagger up here." He used the microphone on Juanita's register to call someone named Chad to the front, and then he wished me a good evening and ambled toward the back of the store.

I knew there hadn't been any love lost between Mr. Franklin and Fred—Mr. Franklin had once spoken to me about how difficult Fred had become after his accident and how he couldn't fire him and risk a lawsuit—but this brusque behavior was inexcusable.

I made a mental note to ask Fran if she knew or could find out why Fred went to Haysi so often and why Mr. Franklin was acting so cold. Could he have been harboring a grudge against Fred that went deeper than Fred's mood swings after the car accident?

## Chapter Three

I got home, put my groceries away and then unpacked the game system and the guitar game Violet wanted me to test. The game controller was a wireless "guitar." I turned it on and started the game's tutorial. It explained to me that "notes" corresponding to the colored buttons serving as frets would scroll down the screen. To play the note, I would hold down the proper fret button and strum the guitar using a long bar that took the place of the guitar's strings. The tutorial sent a few notes my way so I could put this theory into practice. So far, so good.

Next, I got to choose my character. After seeing what—or rather who—my alternatives were, I went with a pouty-mouthed, improperly dressed, tattooed redhead. Cool.

I was ready to play my first song. I was in "easy" mode and I was expecting the song to be . . . well, easy. The music began. Bobbing my head like Jessie—my alter ego—I saw the first note coming at me. Nailed it.

I did fine until we hit the chorus, and then the song sped up. I started missing notes, and the crowd actually began booing me! I was mortified. I quickly went to the menu and restarted the song. I was determined to get it right this time. No way was I going to be booed off the stage my first time out.

No head bobbing this time. This time, I was serious. And I did it. The crowd was cheering wildly. Sure, I missed some notes, but not enough to get booed.

Still, I knew I could do better, so I played that same song again. And again. And again. And then I played the next song...over and over. I didn't stop until an hour later when Myra rang the doorbell.

"What in the world are you doing?" Myra asked.

"Playing a video game Violet wanted me to check out for Lucas. Wanna try it?"

Myra, an attractive woman in her mid-sixties, will generally try anything. This was no exception.

"What do I do?" she asked, picking up the guitar.

I started the tutorial for her, and she was off. I hate to admit it, but her first effort was better than mine.

After she'd played for a few minutes, she said, "You know what we need, don't you? Another guitar. That way, we could both play."

I said I'd stop by the rental place tomorrow and see if they'd rent me another controller.

"Then we can be like those Judds," Myra said. "Or that Billy guy and his girl."

I laughed. "I know you didn't come over to play this game. Did you need something?"

"Actually, I was at Tanya's Tress Tamers today, and I went a little darker with my hair color. What do you think?"

I noticed for the first time since she'd come in that her usually golden hair color had a more honeyed hue. "I like it."

Myra patted her pixie mane. "Do you really?"

"I really do."

"Well, Tanya said that with it being December, I need to go a shade darker until spring. By the way, everybody in the shop was buzzing about poor Fred Duncan. What do you think happened?"

"I don't know. The weird thing is that everyone got sick, everyone took medicine provided by Dr. Holloway, and everyone got better . . . except Fred."

"That's what everybody was buzzing about down at the salon."

"What was the consensus?"

"Some thought Fred's brain injury was why he didn't get better. Some thought maybe Fred didn't take the medicine Dr. Holloway gave out."

"I hadn't considered that."

"And some thought Fred was into something else . . . something illegal . . . and that played a part in his death."

"Something else," I said. "Like drugs?"

Myra shrugged. "I never heard of Fred Duncan being on drugs. I'm just relaying what I heard at the beauty shop."

"What about Haysi?" I asked. "Is there a lot of drug activity around Haysi?"

Myra cocked her head. "Now how should I know? I get all my drugs at the pharmacy. Besides, why Haysi?"

"I saw China in the grocery store, and she mentioned Fred traveled to Haysi on a regular basis."

"Huh." She adjusted the shoulder strap on her guitar. "If you want me to ride with you to Haysi, just say so. Not to scout out drug dealers, but there's a nifty little fabric shop over there."

With that, she started her song again and rocked out. I finally had to tell her I was going to bed before she'd cut the guitar off and leave.

\*

The next morning, Fran, her mother Carol and her Aunt Connie arrived at around 7:45. I had just taken the quiche out of the toaster oven, and biscuits and a coffee cake were baking in the conventional oven. I sat the quiche on a trivet in the center of the table, took off my oven mitts and opened the door.

"Good morning," I said. "Connie, how are you?"

She looked terrible. I don't think she'd had any rest at all, and she appeared weak and fragile.

She managed a smile. "I'm as well as can be expected, I suppose."

Carol rubbed her sister-in-law's back as they came on into the kitchen.

"Is there anything I can help you do?" Fran asked.

Her eagerness to help was evident, so I had her check to see if the biscuits were done. I knew they still needed to bake for three or four more minutes, but that's all I could think of at the moment.

"Connie, Ben Jacobs will be joining us for breakfast," I said. "He stopped by yesterday and expressed to me both his condolences and his concern over Fred's death."

Connie shook her head. "Fred's more than a curiosity for the newspapers."

"I know that. So does Ben." I glanced up and saw his white Jeep pulling into the driveway. "He's here, so please discuss any concerns you have with him. If you don't want to, we'll just have breakfast and not talk about Fred."

Connie merely nodded.

"I think the biscuits are done," Fran said.

"Great," I said, opening the door for Ben. "Could you grab those oven mitts and take them out for me?"

"Sure."

Ben grinned. "I love a busy kitchen."

I laughed. "Sorry it's so crazy this morning. I wanted everything to be done at about the same time so I wouldn't have to reheat anything."

"I'm not complaining," Ben said. He then introduced himself to the others. "I'm terribly sorry for your loss. Please know I'm not here in the capacity of a newspaper reporter but as a friend who wants to discover what caused Fred's death."

"Thank you," Connie said.

I was grateful Ben had tactfully put Fred's family's fears at rest about his being here. I took the coffee cake out of the oven and drizzled butter cream glaze over the top. I then placed the biscuits in a bread basket and moved both over to the table. By each plate, I had sat a juice glass and a coffee cup on a saucer.

"What flavor juice would you like?" I asked. "I have orange and apple."

Everyone voted for orange juice, which I personally felt was a good choice to complement the orange marmalade I had for the biscuits.

I poured the juice and coffee and then ensured everything we might need was on the table prior to sitting down.

"Where do we begin?" Connie asked, taking a sip of her juice.

I took a biscuit and passed the basket to Fran, who was on my left. "I guess we need to start with Fred, you know, see what was going on with him."

"Like what?" Carol asked.

"I understand he frequently went to Haysi. Do any of you know why?" I asked.

"No." Fran attempted to pass her mother the bread basket, but she kept her hands in her lap and addressed me sharply.

"My nephew was not on drugs, if that's what you're getting at."

"I didn't mean to imply that at all," I said. "Maybe Fred has a girlfriend in Haysi. I don't know. All I do know is that Connie asked me to look into Fred's death. If that's no longer the case, I'll be happy to mind my own business."

Connie nudged her sister. "Take a biscuit and simmer down. I did ask Daphne to help me look into Fred's death. That means I want to know the truth . . . no matter what it is."

Carol pressed her lips together and continued to scowl, although she did take a biscuit and pass the basket on to her sister.

Connie took a biscuit and passed the basket to Ben. "Fred did travel quite a bit on his days off. He never said much about his trips, though." She spread margarine on her biscuit. "I didn't want to be nosy, so I didn't ask too many questions. After all, he was a grown man." She shook her head. "I don't think it was a girlfriend. How would he have met her if she lived all the way over in Haysi?"

"An Internet dating site?" Ben suggested. "Or some other social networking type thing?"

"No," Fran said. "Fred wasn't all that into computers. He said they gave him a headache." She took a slice of quiche. "I wonder if he was moonlighting."

"Why would you think that?" Carol asked.

Fran shrugged. "Well, he was upset a few weeks ago about how Mr. Franklin had been treating him at the Save-a-Buck."

I remembered Mr. Franklin's weird behavior from yesterday but didn't feel this was the right time to bring it up.

"And he wanted to get you something really nice for

Christmas, Aunt Connie," Fran continued.

With a nod and a muffled sob, Connie excused herself and hurried into the hall. As Carol shot a disapproving look at Fran—for what, I had no idea—I got up to console Connie and see if she needed tissues or a cool washcloth. Connie gratefully accepted my offer of a cool washcloth and said she'd return to the table momentarily.

When I took my seat, I saw that Ben, Fran and Carol were all eating in awkward silence. I tried to come up with an ice breaker; but every time I looked up from my plate, I met Carol's stony gaze. I determined Ben and Fran had the right idea, and I delved into my breakfast as if I hadn't eaten in days.

Connie returned to the table, her face wan and her eyes puffy. "Sorry I lost it," she said.

Carol put her arm around her sister-in-law's shoulders. "It's okay, sweetie. You have no reason whatsoever to apologize."

I started to agree, but the Ice Queen's frigid glare halted any words from leaving my open mouth.

"Why don't you come over to the house tomorrow and take a look through Fred's room?" Connie asked. "It can't hurt; and if he was seeing someone, maybe you can find her name and phone number. I'd look myself, but I just can't bear to go in there just yet."

"I understand," I said, "and, of course, I'll be happy to do whatever I can to help."

After everyone left, I cleaned up the kitchen. Fran had offered to help, but I insisted that she and her mom needed to get Connie home. Which was true, but I was also eager to be out from under Carol's suspicious glare. What did she have against me? Was she afraid I'd discover something damaging or unsavory about Fred that would cast an even darker shadow over his death? While I thought Fran's suggestion of Fred moonlighting to earn extra money was logical, the thought of him driving all the way to Haysi to do it was not. Haysi was over an hour away—one way—and with the cost of gasoline these days, he'd have to be making quite a bit of money to make it worth the trip.

Connie had said Fred traveled a lot on his days off. I wondered if Haysi was his only destination.

I decided to go out and get the other video game guitar controller since I didn't have any cake orders due today. It would be fun to invite Myra over to play this evening . . . although I was fairly certain there were no Judds' songs on the game.

It was a gorgeous day for early December. The sun was shining and it was warm enough outside that a light jacket was sufficient. I was wearing jeans, a red turtleneck and a jean jacket as I walked down the street, and I was perfectly comfortable. I passed Tanya's Tress Tamers and waved a hello to Tanya. Her daughter was graduating high school this year; and the last time I was in Tanya's shop for a trim, she talked about ordering a cake for the big day. I realize that's six months away, but I hadn't given much thought to graduation cakes before Tanya mentioned it. Tanya is the type of mom who plans things well in advance.

Hopefully, I'd get several orders for graduation cakes. At least, I could count on making a few for Save-A-Buck. I'd have to go home and dig out my May/June cake magazines and idea books.

As I continued walking, Cara came out of the café with a lidded cup of coffee. "Daphne, hi. Have you got a sec?"

I glanced at my watch as if I had somewhere to be. Somehow being in such close proximity to someone as accomplished as Cara made me want to act as if I had a lot on the ball. "I have a few minutes."

"That's terrif," she said, taking my arm and tugging me toward the café.

See how busy she is? She doesn't even have time to finish three-syllable words like 'terrific.'

"Come sit with me, grab a java and let's dish."

I don't know why Cara's suggestion made me feel nervous and reluctant today. Maybe I was afraid I'd say something completely stupid and then wind up seeing it in print tomorrow morning. I checked my watch one more time.

"Come on," she said. "The fondant will wait."

I smiled. "Like I said, I can spare a few minutes." I sat down at a nearby table. "How do you like Brea Ridge?"

Cara sat opposite me. "It's quaint." She pushed her perfectly-highlighted hair out of her eyes with her perfectly-manicured red-tipped fingers. "Charming." She smiled. "Really."

"Oh, you don't have to convince me," I said. "How's your story coming along?"

"Good and bad." She took a drink of her coffee and signaled the waitress. "We need to get you fixed up with one of these. It isn't Starbuck's by any stretch, but it's not half bad. Besides, I hate to drink alone."

The waitress came over and Cara ordered me a French vanilla cappuccino "just like mine, love. And put a rush on it, would you please?"

The waitress hurried off to get my cappuccino. Hopefully, since Cara had added "please" to the rush order, the waitress wouldn't spit in it. I've always been careful about how I treat wait staff . . . especially before I get my food. But again, Cara had said "please" and she'd called the young woman "love" with only the slightest hint of condescension.

"Okay," Cara said, "back to the story. The one guy who didn't get better after taking the drug administered at the party died, which is good from a personal interest standpoint; but it's bad from a Brea Ridge Pharmaceuticals PR standpoint."

"So are you killing the story for the benefit of Brea Ridge Pharmaceuticals and Dr. Holloway?" I asked.

The waitress returned with my cappuccino, and I thanked her before turning back to Cara expectantly.

"What? You were serious?" she asked. "The story must be told. Always. That's just how it is."

"But what about Dr. Holloway? Won't that cause problems between the two of you?"

She shrugged. "He has his job, and I have mine. We must be vigilant not to allow our relationship to affect our jobs. And vice versa. Of course."

"Of course. Do you think I could talk with Dr. Holloway?" I asked. "I'd love to get his opinion on what happened to Fred Duncan."

"You're not trying to scoop me, are you?" She asked the question jokingly and with a smile on her face, but there was a steely glint in her brown eyes.

"Not at all. You're the writer. I'm happy decorating cakes." I took a drink of cappuccino. "I'm curious, that's all."

"Well, I can assure you my article will answer all your questions. I'll send you a couple copies. You did get the ones I sent you about the Oklahoma Sugar Arts Show, didn't you?"

"I did. Thank you. The article was terrific."

She leaned back in her chair. "It was a good piece, wasn't it?" She pushed her hair back from her face again. "That was a fun event. Are you going back this year? And entering a cake this time?"

"I'm considering it."

"You should do it. Even if you don't win—and you very well might—it's fabulous publicity."

I nodded. "How about your friend? I can't remember her name."

"Ellen?"

"Yes. How did she do? My flight left before the judging."

"She did well. She got a few words of high praise from HRH Kerry Vincent. And she was able to parlay that into some local and national publicity. She's hoping to be invited onto that cake challenge show."

"Oh, that would be cool."

"Tell me about it. It's launched more than one career, you know." She leaned forward, interlacing her fingers. "I've got the number of a fab publicist who could work up a campaign for you."

"Um . . . wow . . . thanks. Maybe I can look into that after the holidays."

"You need to if you're ever going to take it to the next level, Daphne. I'll call you later with the number."

"Great. Thank you." I sipped my cappuccino. I didn't share Cara's ambitious nature. I'm not really a spotlight kinda gal. I'd prefer to live my life quietly and peacefully. I had enough excitement while I was married to the human volcano. But I'd be polite and take the number. I'd said *maybe* I could look into it after the holidays. I didn't commit to anything, and I hadn't even specified which holidays.

"Remember that cake at the show that had been damaged?" I asked. "There was a card on the table indicating the cake had been damaged by a spectator."

"I remember that," Cara said. "Some of the lattice trim or something had been torn off."

"Right. And it was such a gorgeous cake." I shook my head slowly. "I could've cried for the decorator."

"Oh, love, that guy was such a jerk. He was so terribly snotty to Ellen and to everyone else who was unfortunate enough to cross his path . . . even Mrs. Vincent."

"Still, I know how hard he had to have worked on that cake. Then to have someone ruin it and knock him out of the competition had to have been heartbreaking."

"Yeah, I guess," Cara said. "But everyone worked hard on their entries. You know?" She shrugged. "And everyone knows the risks."

The waitress stopped by our table to see if we needed anything else.

"No thanks, love," Cara said. "We're leaving." She opened her purse, took out a $20 bill and dropped it onto the table. "Keep the change." She tossed her head and ran her hand though her hair one final time. "I'm so glad we got a chance to catch up, Daphne. I'll call you later this afternoon."

I smiled. "Thank you for the cappuccino." Although I did feel that plunking down twenty dollars for a coffee and a tip was a bit over the top in extravagance, I kept mum. "Take care."

She laughed. "Always, love. Always."

After renting the second guitar controller, I went straight to Ben's office. The grandmotherly receptionist, who watched too many hours of daytime drama which played on the set in the lobby, smiled slyly.

"You're here to see your beau?" she asked.

How was I supposed to answer a question like that? Was I supposed to say, "Yes, ma'am, tell my honey I'm here?" Or was I supposed to be honest and tell her, "I'm not altogether certain Ben and I have reached the beau/belle relationship status." Instead, I circumvented the issue.

"Ben isn't expecting me," I said. "If he's too busy to see me, that's fine."

"Oh, I doubt he's ever too busy to see you. Have you been practicing wedding cakes?"

"No."

"You'd better hop to it."

Since Ben had survived for the past forty years without walking down the aisle—or, I suppose, standing at the end of an aisle—I didn't see the need to rush out and buy a cake topper just yet . . . even if I was ready to take that step myself—which evidently was neither here nor there in the eyes of Granny Newspaper Office Matchmaker.

She called Ben and told him I was there. She then hung up and instructed me to go on back.

I went down the hall to Ben's office and he met me at the door.

"Getting to see you twice today before noon," he said. "How did I get so lucky?"

"Have you spoken with Dr. Holloway of Brea Ridge Pharmaceuticals?"

He nodded and ushered me into his office. "I spoke with him just after I left your house this morning."

I sat down on one of the chairs in front of his desk, and he sat on the other.

"I ran into Cara Logan this morning."

"The reporter from Richmond?" he asked.

"Yeah. She was coming out of the café and wanted to chat."

"Did she share any information?"

"Not much. And when I asked about speaking with Dr. Holloway, she told me her article will answer all my questions. She acted like I was trying to scoop her."

"That's silly. You wouldn't do that." He grinned. "But I would. Besides, I don't know how she can be completely objective since she's dating John Holloway."

"I don't think that's a problem for Cara. In fact, she seemed to like the fact that Fred's death added to the personal interest aspect of the story, even if it does look bad for Brea Ridge Pharmaceuticals."

Ben shook his head. "She sounds like a lovely person."

"She can be nice," I said. "At least, she was in Oklahoma. But she's very driven."

"Sounds like it."

"So what did you learn from Dr. Holloway?"

"They'd been working on a drug to quickly combat the effects of gastroenteritis."

"What's that?"

"Stomach flu."

"But aren't there already a lot of those types of drugs on the market?" I asked.

"Apparently none that work as quickly as this one, barring IVs."

"What a coincidence they had this on hand when everyone fell ill at the Christmas party. Looks pretty suspicious to me."

"I made that same observation," Ben said, "but Holloway seemed to have been genuinely surprised when the people at the party became ill."

"You said they were working on this drug. It hadn't been approved yet?"

"Yes and no. Brea Ridge Pharmaceuticals had been performing various clinical trials with the drug, and it's due to be released as a prescription drug shortly after the first of the year."

"So the party attendees weren't the first test subjects for this drug," I said.

"No. The product had already been widely tested. Fred is

the only person who died after taking it."

"Did Dr. Holloway offer any speculation about why Fred was adversely affected?"

"He has no clue . . . unless Fred was allergic to some component of the drug, which Holloway feels is unlikely," Ben said. "And unlike his girlfriend, he seems to feel genuinely bad about Fred . . . and I don't mean because of the legal hassles this will prompt. The guy is in the business of saving lives. He thought dispensing that drug the other evening was a heroic action."

"Are there any drug interactions that have an adverse effect when taken with this drug?" I asked.

"None that they're currently aware of."

"Did Dr. Holloway ask the people if they were currently taking any meds or had known drug allergies prior to dispensing the drug?"

"He did. He also had them sign waivers. Well, I think they more literally initialed the waivers," Ben said. "Most of them weren't physically able to sign their names."

"Ugh. Why didn't they rush the people to the hospital rather than doing on-the-spot first aid?"

"They did call an ambulance. While they were awaiting paramedics, they administered the new drug. By the time the ambulance arrived, seventy-five percent of the people affected were feeling some better." Ben spread his hands. "Everyone else—with the exception of Fred, of course—recovered completely within twenty-four hours."

"Wow. Whatever the drug is, it must be a hundred times better than the over-the-counter stuff."

"I guess so. Brea Ridge Pharmaceuticals stands to make billions off it. Or, at least, they did."

"So now what?"

"Now they have to see what the fallout from this incident will be."

"Is Dr. Holloway optimistic?" I asked.

"He's guarded. He's waiting for Fred's autopsy report to see what that reveals."

"Was he guarded when he talked with you?"

"No. He was open and candid. He did ask me to refrain from painting Brea Ridge Pharmaceuticals in a bad light to the best of my ability."

"What did you say to that?" I asked.

"I told him I certainly didn't want to portray Brea Ridge Pharmaceuticals negatively and that I would report the facts objectively," he said. "And I told him I'd report the fact that he and Brea Ridge Pharmaceuticals are working diligently to learn what happened to cause Fred Duncan's death."

"That's good." I sighed. "I feel so sorry for Fred's family. You know they're thinking, 'Why Fred?'"

"I know. But, then, that's what we're all wondering. Isn't it?"

Chapter Four

After leaving the newspaper offices, I was ready to go home, rock out and lose myself in a virtual world for a little while. Then I got home and checked my messages. Mr. Franklin had called with eight more cake orders—four birthday and four seasonal. Cara had called with the name and number of the publicist I "absolutely *have*" to call. And Belinda Fremont, who has the prize-winning guinea pigs, wanted to talk with me about catering a New Year's Eve affair.

The video game would have to wait. I decided to unwind by losing myself in butter cream. Belinda would also have to wait, for at least an hour or so. Cara's publicist would have to wait longer . . . much, much longer.

Eight cakes. Mr. Franklin hadn't specified what kinds—other than four birthday and four seasonal. I had two white round cakes in the freezer, along with two chocolate quarter sheet cakes. I sat those out to thaw. For two of the cakes, I decided to prepare a pumpkin crème cake with cream cheese filling and vanilla butter cream frosting.

I got out my favorite blue mixing bowl, my whisk, my pumpkin crème cake recipe and the necessary ingredients. I put my phone headset on, turned on the radio and began singing Christmas carols while I worked. Soon the kitchen smelled like pumpkin and vanilla, and my soul was content.

While the pumpkin cakes were baking, I mixed up two marble cakes and poured those into the pans. Then I put the ingredients for a double batch of vanilla butter cream in my stand mixer bowl.

The phone rang and I answered, "Daphne's Delectable Cakes. How may I help you?"

"Daphne, it's Fran. Sorry about how my mom acted this morning."

"Oh, sweetheart, that's fine. She's only concerned about your aunt."

"I know," Fran said, "but sometimes she can be a little over the top."

I chuckled. "All moms can be."

"Thank you for breakfast. Everything was delicious. I wish I could cook like you."

"Thank you."

"Instead of tomorrow, would you care to go with me to Aunt Connie's house later this afternoon?" she asked. "The funeral home is having Aunt Connie come to view Fred's body at four-thirty to make sure he looks okay . . . or something. Mom is taking Aunt Connie over there, so I thought that might be a good time for us to begin investigating. What do you think?"

"Is it all right with your Aunt Connie?"

"Yeah, sure, it's fine. I asked her. Only I didn't let Mom hear me."

I didn't blame her, but I refrained from saying so. "Shall I meet you there then?"

"Or I could come by and pick you up at around four," she said.

"All right. I'll see you at four."

"Good deal."

After talking with Fran and while keeping butter cream off the sides of the mixing bowl with a silicone spatula, I returned Belinda's call.

"Daphne, darling, how are you?" she asked.

"I'm doing well. And you?"

"I'm excited. As you already know from the message I left you earlier, I'm hosting a New Year's Eve soiree. Of course, I'll need something for the people and something for the cavies. Can you come by sometime tomorrow to discuss?"

"I certainly can. Morning or afternoon?"

"Let's do one-thirty, but we'll have to be quiet. The babies go down for their naps at one p.m."

The "babies" are, naturally, Belinda's champion Satin Peruvian guinea pigs. "I'll be all tiptoes and whispers," I said.

"Great. And bring not only your ideas about cakes but

also about dessert bars and cold buffet foods . . . maybe hot buffet foods, too. We'll see what we come up with when we put our heads together."

*

By the time the four freshly baked cakes had cooled enough—and the four previously frozen cakes had warmed enough—to be crumb coated, it was two-thirty. By the time I'd crumb coated all eight cakes, Fran was pulling into my driveway. She knocked on the kitchen door as I was cleaning up.

"Come on in," I said. "Can you give me five minutes?"

"No problem. Anything I can do to help?"

"Nope. I've almost got it." I followed her confused stare to the eight crumb-coated cakes sitting on cake stands on the island in the center of the kitchen. "Don't worry," I said with a laugh. "I'm not leaving them like that. That's a crumb coat."

"Oh, sure. Yeah."

I could tell she still had no idea what I was talking about. "It's like a paint primer . . . or a base coat when you polish your nails. When I get back, I'll put another layer of frosting on the cake; and the cakes will be even and crumb free."

She turned and smiled at me. "I get it now. Cool."

I finished putting bowls, spoons and spatulas into the dishwasher. Then I threw away the waxed paper I'd been using as a tablecloth and ran a kitchen wipe over the counter.

"All done," I said. "Ready to go?"

"Yeah. And we'll probably need to be finished at Aunt Connie's house by five o'clock."

I cocked my head. "Are you sure your Aunt Connie knows we're coming?"

"She does. But Mom doesn't."

"Don't you think we should tell her?" I asked.

"Later, maybe. Not tonight, though. We'd better go."

Although still a little hesitant given the fact that Fran's mother wasn't on board with our investigation—and neither was my sister, for that matter—I went on with Fran. After all, Connie knew Fran and I would be there; and she was desperate to know what had happened to her son. I felt I owed it to her and to Fran to help find out, if I could.

The house was still and quiet when Fran unlocked the door and we walked in. I hadn't expected it to be loud and lively, of course, but the air of sadness and gloom hung in the house like a thick fog. Somewhere a clock ticked, a constant reminder of time's limits and preciousness.

Fran flipped a switch, but the ensuing overhead light did little to expel the gloom. The room had dark wood paneling and dark furniture. I wondered if I'd have found it cozy under different circumstances. Somehow, I didn't think so.

"Fred's room is this way," Fran said.

I followed her down a narrow hallway lined on both sides with pictures of Fred at various stages of his life. In high school, he'd evidently been quite the athlete: baseball, football, basketball. There was even a photo of Fred as a member of a bowling league. I wondered—not for the first time, but more intensely now—how Fred's car accident had affected his life . . . how it had affected Connie's life.

Fran led me into a room cluttered with clothes, sketchbooks and magazines featuring athletes and reptiles. I was struck by the fact that there were no video game systems in the room. Maybe his brain injury had prevented him from playing video games. Fran had said computers gave Fred a headache.

Fran turned on the lamp which sat on Fred's nightstand, and I got a better view of the room. There was a shelf on the wall across from the neatly-made bed that held an array of trophies. The dresser held a small television set, another trophy and an aquarium containing Fred's ball python Rusty.

Fred must have had such a promising future before the accident. Not that he didn't have a promising future after the accident, but this was not the room of a young man whose dream was to bag groceries at Save-A-Buck for the rest of his life.

"I never knew Fred was so invested in sports," I said.

"Yeah," Fran said, running her finger gently over the

nameplate of the trophy on the dresser. "He was something."

"We don't have to do this right now."

She sniffled. "We need to. Let's get it done." She wiped her nose on the back of her hand. "What are we looking for?"

"An address book, notebook, phone numbers, business cards . . . anything like that." I picked up a sketchbook from off the nightstand and began thumbing through it. The sketches were mostly of cars, and I knew I didn't have time to look through it carefully. "Can we take this with us? We can look it over at my house, and you can bring it back."

Fran looked over her shoulder. "Yeah, that's fine. What about this?" She held up a small, black, spiral-bound notepad. "It has some writing in it."

"Yeah," I said. "Let's take anything that might have potential back to my house where we'll have time to look it over. You can return it later this evening." At her troubled expression, I added, "Or, you know, at your discretion."

"Okay." She looked relieved.

I understood. Sneak it out; sneak it back in. Mom is none the wiser. That one gave me a momentary twinge of guilt, but I had a speedy recovery. I felt Carol had been a tad harsh with Fran at breakfast; although, admittedly, having no children of my own left me in no position to pass judgment.

I didn't find any business cards or scraps of paper with phone numbers written on them. Neither did Fran. We decided Fred would have likely kept anything like that which was important to him in his wallet. And we had no idea where that was.

I was also disappointed that we didn't find a calendar or day planner. In the end, we wound up taking only a couple sketchbooks and the black notebook back to my house for closer inspection.

When Fran and I got back to my house, I made us both a decaf café au lait with whipped cream and cinnamon. I put on my favorite instrumental jazz CD so the kitchen wouldn't be too quiet as we poured over the sketchbooks and the notebook.

We decided to go through the sketchbooks first. I was hoping that if Fred did have a girlfriend in Haysi or anywhere else, there would be some sketches of her.

In the book I had, there was a drawing of Rusty, the python, lying on the rock in his aquarium. There was also a terrific likeness of Fran.

"Look," I said, turning the book around toward Fran. "This is great. Fred really could draw."

"Yeah." Fran smiled slightly. "I remember when he did this one. It was back in August. I'd been over there helping Aunt Connie make apple butter. My hair frizzes really bad when it's humid out—like that day—and I was complaining about it." She closed her eyes momentarily. "He told me I just couldn't see myself realistically. And then he drew this."

"Why don't you ask Connie if you can have it? If she says yes, I'll take it to Johnson City and get it matted and framed for you."

"I'll do that," she said. "Thank you."

There were several sketches of cars . . . or, more accurately, a car. It was a black four-door sedan of ambiguous make and model. In some drawings, the car appeared to be in good condition. In others, it was wrecked. In one drawing, the car was on fire.

"What's with this car?" I asked Fran. "Is this the car Fred was driving when he had his accident?"

She shook her head. "It's not the car *he* was driving. It's the car the drunk driver was in."

"Was the other driver convicted?"

"No, he was never found. He left the scene of the accident. Plus, nobody showed up at any of the local hospitals that night or the next day for treatment for injuries sustained in a car accident."

"How about the car?"

"It was never found either."

"That's a shame. Poor Fred."

"Yeah. It made him angry that the other driver was never found."

"I can imagine. How did police come to the conclusion the other driver was drunk?"

"Someone had reported the guy a few minutes before the accident. The car was swerving all over the road." She rubbed her eyes. "The fact that the guy ran was also fairly damning."

"Were there any witnesses to the accident?"

"The man who'd reported the car weaving had turned off the road and pulled into his driveway. As he was walking to the door, he heard the crash. He jumped back in his car and went to the scene of the accident, but he only saw Fred's car smashed against the telephone pole. The other car was speeding away."

"The man didn't get the car's license tag?" I asked. "Not even when he called police with the initial report?"

"No. Their cars were too far apart. The man who called and reported the guy on suspicion of drunk driving had been afraid to get close enough to get a tag number. He was scared the guy would cause him to wreck." She sighed. "Besides, he thought police would be able to stop him before he did much damage. It wasn't a heavily trafficked road."

"So is that why Fred kept drawing this particular type of car?"

She needed. "He always said he'd recognize it if he ever saw it again."

We went back to flipping through the drawings. There was a rough sketch of the birthday cake Fred had wanted me to make for his grandfather. It was a round cake with a snake's body wrapped around the middle and its head resting atop the cake.

The emotional impact of that sketch hit me hard. I quickly scooted my chair back from the table so my tears wouldn't fall on Fred's work.

"Are you okay?" Fran asked.

"Yeah . . . I just . . . . Could you hand me a napkin please?"

She took a napkin from the rack in the center of the table and gave it to me. I wiped my eyes.

"Sorry," I said. "That sketch got to me, that's all. I

remember when Fred called and asked me to make this cake." This prompted fresh tears, so Fran handed me another napkin. She took one for herself as well.

"I still want to make this cake," I said. "For free. For Fred. I'd like to make it for your grandfather on his birthday, so he'll know how much he meant to Fred."

"He'd appreciate that," Fran said.

We returned to looking at the drawings in silence until a couple minutes later when Fran said, "Well, look at that."

"What is it?" I asked.

"Given how you felt about the cake picture, this one will really blow you away." She turned the book toward me.

"It's me."

It was my face almost in profile, looking down slightly. My expression was soft and pensive. It was as if he'd drawn it from a photograph.

I covered my mouth with my hand. When I glanced up at Fran, she was crying softly. I closed both books.

"That's enough for this evening," I said. "Let's go into the living room."

We moved to the living room where I curled up on the club chair and Fran sat on the sofa. After a few minutes of sitting in silence, I asked Fran if she was all right.

"Yeah," she said. "It's just tough, you know. Fred was a good guy. His dad died when he was ten, and after that Fred always tried to be a grown up. He didn't deserve any of this."

"I know, Fran. I'm so sorry."

"Me, too."

"Do you still want to investigate?" I asked. "I know the police are doing everything they can, and—"

"No. I want to do this. I need to do this."

"Okay, then. I'll try to help you find answers."

\*

After Fran left, I put the second layer of frosting on the cakes and placed them in the refrigerator. I'd decorate them tomorrow.

I heated up a can of tomato soup and then poured it into a

mug. I sat on a stool at the island and opened Fred's notebook. There wasn't much information in it. I sipped my soup and tried to make sense of the scant notes.

"SAB 4-10 MWTF, 8-1 SS."

I figured that was Fred's schedule at the Save-A-Buck.

"HMRA – T – 11."

I made a mental note to look that acronym up on the computer after I'd finished my soup. I flipped the pages and came across Rusty's feeding schedule. It nearly made me gag on my soup to read that Rusty had ingested a thawed mouse only four days ago. I remembered Fred once telling me he bought Rusty frozen mice to eat. As incredible as it sounds, live rodents can sometimes hurt snakes.

I got up to retrieve my cordless phone and to pour the remainder of my soup down the sink. Fran answered her cell phone on the first ring.

"Hi, Fran. It's Daphne. I found Rusty's feeding schedule in Fred's notebook."

"Great. I checked the small freezer in Aunt Connie's garage, and there are still a few mice in there."

"Eww," I said.

She giggled. "You get used to it. When was Rusty's latest meal?"

"Four days ago."

"Good. That'll hold him for about another week and a half."

"Hey, does the acronym HMRA mean anything to you?"

"Afraid not," Fran said.

"Oh, well. We'll figure it out later."

"Okay. Thanks for calling about Rusty."

We hung up, and I headed for my office. Before I could get there, though, the doorbell rang.

I went to the living room and opened the door. Myra was standing there in a pink track suit and sneakers.

"Did you get it?" she asked. "Did you get the other remote?"

I grinned. "I got it. Are you ready to rock?"

"I am about to rock. Salute me!"

I laughed as Myra came inside.

"Am I interrupting anything?" she asked.

"No. I was getting ready to try to find an acronym on the computer, but this will be way more fun."

"What acronym? Maybe I'll know what it is."

"It's HMRA," I said. "Does it sound familiar?"

"Did you say '*H*MRA' or '*A*MRA'?"

"'H' as in happy. Have you heard of it?"

"I've heard of AMRA. That's Abingdon Medical Research Association. Yodel Watson once went up there and took a round of weight loss drugs. They didn't work though." She frowned. "Of course, all those Watsons were always big people, and I reckon it was just their cross to bear that they stay that way. I heard that one time the doctor put one of those belly band things on Yodel's sister Harmony. They told her to stick to liquids for a few days."

"How did she do?" I asked.

"Oh, honey. She went straight home and put biscuits and sausage gravy in the blender, and she lived off that stuff and chocolate milkshakes. I heard that when she went back for her first checkup, she'd broke that belly band half in two."

"Is that even possible?"

Myra shrugged. "I'm only telling you what I heard. Now, are we gonna jam or what?"

"We're gonna jam," I said, getting the game set up.

"Good. Who's your person?"

"I'm Jessie Lax. Who do you want to be?"

"I want you to show me all of them so I can decide."

In the end, Myra chose über Goth Lizzie Bourdain because "they call her guitar an axe, and it's fancy."

Chapter Five

The first thing I did when I got up the next morning was set out the eight cakes I needed to decorate. I put the cakes, the butter cream and the fondant on the island; and then I made myself a bowl of cereal. I felt guilty the entire time I was eating my cereal, though, because I could hear Sparrow on the porch crying for her breakfast.

After eating and putting my bowl and spoon into the dishwasher, I pulled my plush yellow robe embellished with daisy appliqués tighter around myself and braved the cool December morning air with Sparrow's food. She must've been starving because she didn't run away and wait until she was positive I'd gone inside before returning. This morning, she dug right in with me still standing there beside her. I bent slightly and stroked her head. She didn't purr, but she didn't run away either. I smiled to myself as I went inside to shower and dress. Sparrow and I were definitely making progress.

After I'd dressed and had my second cup of coffee, I was ready to face the day. I decided to start with the four birthday cakes. I had some flavored fondant I'd ordered at the Oklahoma Sugar Art Show—fondant has a yearlong shelf life, by the way, when stored in airtight packaging—and I wanted to use the fondant to make some fun birthday cake decorations. I had grape, tutti-frutti, strawberry and white chocolate.

As I formed 3D balloons using the grape, tutti-frutti and strawberry fondant, I found myself thinking about Fred's funeral. The funeral was taking place at eleven o'clock tomorrow morning. I wondered if Mr. Franklin would attend. I wondered if he'd allow his employees to attend. Surely, the man would be decent enough to at least send flowers.

What was his problem anyway? I realized he had issues with Fred, but people generally put their petty differences aside at a time like this. Don't they?

Mr. Franklin had always struck me as a reasonable,

somewhat kind man. Could his gruff demeanor simply be hiding his grief?

I placed the balloons on one of the round cakes and then attached blue-colored string piping. I piped top and bottom borders and then wrote "Happy Birthday" on the cake in green script. One down, seven to go.

For the next birthday cake, I decided to make ribbon roses using the strawberry fondant.

Luckily, I'd remembered to put on my headset because China York called.

"Good morning," I said. "How are you?"

"I'm fit as a fiddler on the Fourth of July," she said. "Are you busy?"

"I'm never too busy for you."

"Good. I want you to make me a Christmas cake."

"What flavor would you like?"

"Chocolate, I reckon, with vanilla icing."

"All right. How would you like it decorated?"

"I want either a Bible or a cross. We aim to remember the reason for the season, you know."

"I can make it a sheet cake with a Bible and a cross on it if you want me to."

"Nah, I don't reckon we need to be tacky about it."

I pressed my lips together to keep from giggling. When I regained my composure, I said, "I have a cake pan in the shape of a cross. What do you think of that?"

"Why, I'd like that fine. Can I get me some purple roses on it? Purple represents royalty, you know."

"I'll put a cluster of roses right in the center. Would you like me to write 'Merry Christmas' on it?"

"No, I want you to write 'Happy Birthday' on it. I always make Jesus a birthday cake; but I figure since you can probably use the work, I'll let you do it this year."

"Thank you," I said. "I appreciate that."

"Can I pick it up on the 24th?"

"If that's when you want it, that's when I'll have it."

"I'll pick it up that morning then. So, how's your

investigation into Fred's murder coming along?"

That one threw me. "Murder?"

"Well, sure. You don't reckon it was an accident or a coincidence or some other nonsense that all them people got sick at the same time, do you?"

"I . . . I don't know."

"Of course, you do. You just ain't ready to own up to it yet. Well, I'd better go. Let me know if you need anything."

"Wait," I said. "Have you heard anything about why Mr. Franklin from the Save-A-Buck is acting so weird about Fred's death?"

"I've not heard anything; but from what I've seen, Steve Franklin is acting like a man with a guilty conscience."

"You don't think he contaminated the food at the Brea Ridge Christmas party, do you?"

"No, but something about Fred is eating at that man. Maybe it's because he demoted Fred after Yodel Watson made that stink about the produce department being unorganized a while back." She clucked her tongue. "I don't know what it is he's feeling guilty about, but I know he's feeling guilty. I've seen enough people carrying around that burden to know it when I see it."

"Huh."

"I'll let you get back to work now," China said, "and I'll do the same."

As soon as we hung up, I wrote down her cake order and delivery date.

Could China be right? Was Steve Franklin suffering from guilt over something concerning Fred's death?

\*

After decorating the cakes for Save-A-Buck and placing them in *Daphne's Delectable Cakes* boxes, I sat down with a stack of magazines and catalogs to get some ideas for Belinda's New Year's Eve party.

Dessert bars are a growing trend. One magazine article stated, "Good options are desserts that are portable and not too sticky so guests can take their desserts, mingle and then return." The same magazine stated that cupcake towers and petit four towers are also gaining popularity. Some people like to include a monogram or initial on their petit fours.

*Belinda Fremont would love white petit-fours with the initial F in gold*, I thought. I wrote that suggestion down on my notepad.

The article suggested mini pies and tarts to provide an alternative to cakes and candies. Themed cookies were another suggestion.

I made notes on all of this. I was guessing that—knowing Belinda from her guinea pig Guinevere's birthday party—she was going to want some of all of the above for both her human guests and her cavies. I went to my office and booted up the computer. Somehow I was afraid organic cookie recipes for guinea pigs might be hard to come by, but you'd be surprised at how quickly I found a recipe for "vegetarian biscuits" for guinea pigs. The author said she developed the recipe by combining a carrot cake recipe with a recipe for scones. Go figure. You really can find anything on the Internet.

\*

I was preparing my portfolio to take to Belinda's house when the phone rang.

"Daphne's Delectable Cakes," I answered. "How can I help you have a sweet day?"

"This is so unfair!"

"Fran? Is that you?"

"Yes, and I'm so mad at my mom."

"Are you driving?" I asked. Teens on the phone while driving are scary enough. Angry teens on the phone while driving make me want to hide under the bed. Dust bunnies notwithstanding.

"No," she said. "I'm in the parking lot at the mall. I need to find a black dress for tomorrow."

"Okay, good. Are your doors locked? Because I don't want some thief catching you unaware and either rob you or jack your car while we're talking."

"I'm locking the doors now."

I heard the click and felt relieved.

"Wow," Fran continued, "you really take this crime stuff seriously, don't you?"

"Well, not to sound like your mother, but 'better safe than sorry' is a cliché for a reason."

"Speaking of her, I am so totally mad at her. She says she's not letting me help you with the investigation into Fred's death anymore."

"Really? Did she say why?"

"She thinks you're a busybody and that you're only doing this to help your boyfriend score another popular newspaper article."

"No, really," I said, "tell me how she truly feels. I can take it."

"That *is* how she feels!"

"Fran, I was being sarcastic. It's okay."

"It's *not* okay! How can she do this to me? This is important to me, and I'm not gonna let her ruin it! She ruins everything!"

"Calm down," I said. "It's not that bad."

"It is totally that bad! She's never wanted me to be a criminologist, but she cannot stop me from pursuing my dream. She can't!"

"Would you please hear me out?" I asked softly.

"Yeah, sure. I'm sorry."

"How would your mom feel about your helping me prepare to cater a party for Belinda Fremont?"

"*The* Belinda Fremont . . . with the mansion and the award-winning hamsters?"

"Guinea pigs, actually. Satin Peruvian guinea pigs."

"Are you serious? About the catering, I mean."

"Yes. I would get the help I desperately need with this party, you would learn something about baking and make a few bucks, and we could—when we have time—compare notes on the investigation."

"All *right*."

"Don't mention this to your mom yet," I said. "I'll ask her permission for you to be my paid assistant—" I affected a haughty accent. "—with regard to the Fremont affair." I returned to my normal voice. "In the meantime, you go home and make nice with your mom."

"Got it. You so rock, Daphne."

We hung up and I picked up my portfolio and headed out the door. The last thing I wanted to do was come between Fran and her mother. But I really did need help with Belinda's party, and maybe the arrangement would placate Fran and help her feel she was still in the investigation "loop." I wasn't even sure I was in the investigation loop—or that I wanted to be—but, at least, Fran would know as much as I did.

It's bemusing how the name "Belinda Fremont" opens so many doors in Brea Ridge. Of course, when I got to Belinda's house, I remembered why.

Belinda's home is modeled after Crane Cottage on Jekyll Island, Georgia. It's an elegant, white home patterned after an Italian Renaissance villa. Belinda's house even copies the enclosed courtyard with formal garden surrounded by arcaded loggias.

I pulled up to the gate and pressed the intercom button. "Daphne Martin to see Mrs. Fremont."

Belinda's gatekeeper/assistant—whom I'd once mistaken for her husband—replied, "Mrs. Fremont is expecting you, Ms. Martin. Please come on in."

The gate slowly opened, granting me entrance into the fairytale kingdom. I drove onto the white and terra cotta brick mosaic drive. The last time I was here it was to deliver cakes for Guinevere's birthday party—one cake for the human guests, and one for the guinea pigs and their guests. You see, Guinevere, Lancelot, Morgan, Arthur, Beatrice and Merlin are the champion Satin Peruvian guinea pigs. They have their own suite on the second floor. I'm hoping they'll invite me to a sleepover sometime.

I never cease to be impressed by Belinda Fremont's poise and put-together appearance. Maybe she has what some people call an "old soul," because even though she's only about 35, she has the sophistication and polish of someone older. I wish

I had that much sophistication, and I'm lucky to get polish on my nails once in awhile.

Unlike my first meeting with Belinda, I didn't bring cake samples. As I quietly explained to her (it's nap time for the cavies, you know) when we'd sat down in her Victorian inspired parlor with the uncomfortable Louis Quatorze furniture, I'd prefer to get her ideas for the dessert bar and then bring samples next week so she can see how the flavors will mesh.

"Very good," she said. "But early next week. How about Tuesday morning at eleven-thirty?"

"That'll be great." I penciled the date and time in my notebook.

"So what are my options?" Belinda asked.

"Naturally, there will be a variety of fresh fruits for both the cavies and the humans," I said, remembering how important Vitamin C is to a cavy's diet.

"Naturally."

"I also found a recipe for cavy cookies."

Belinda clapped her hands. "That's wonderful! My darlings have never had cookies before."

"I'll bring them a sample when I come back on Tuesday so they can decide whether or not they like them. If they're not happy with them, I'll modify the recipe."

Belinda smiled broadly. "Excellent."

I went on to outline the current trends. I was correct in thinking Belinda would adore white petit-fours with gold Fs on them. She also wanted a mini cake tower and a mini tart tower. As for the cake, she requested a "simple three-tier affair with sparklers in the top."

I told her I'd be happy to oblige and that I'd ask the fire department to be on standby.

"Oh, Daphne, what a wit you have," Belinda said with a laugh. "Oh, and I'll need some things that are sugar free. Richard's sister is coming, and she's a diabetic."

"Would you like the cake to be sugar free?"

She flipped one thin wrist. "One tier, perhaps. Either the

top or middle . . . but be sure and let me know which it is. Maureen doesn't need a great deal of cake. She's single again, and Richard is hoping this will help her meet some people."

"All right," I said. "Anything else I should know?"

"I think that should do it . . . at least, until we talk again on Tuesday."

*

I was on my way to the Save-A-Buck to deliver the cakes when my cell phone rang. It was Ben.

"Hi, beautiful," he said. "Would you like to go with me to Dakota's tomorrow night?"

"I'd love to." Dakota's is the only steakhouse in Brea Ridge. It's independently owned and, during the summer, the proprietor buys the restaurant's produce from local farmers. Even now some of the items on the menu—apple butter and peach chutney for the biscuits, for instance—were made and canned locally.

"I thought we'd need a pick-me-up after Fred's funeral tomorrow," Ben said.

"Thank you. You're awfully thoughtful, you know."

"Oh, I know." He chuckled.

"By the way," I said, "could you look in your archive room and make me a copy of any articles mentioning Fred's car accident?"

"Why do you want that?"

"Just curious. Fran was telling me about the accident, and I'd like to see a more timely account."

"I probably wrote the articles myself, Daph. What do you want to know?"

"I'd like to read the eyewitness' testimony, that's all."

"All right. I'll dig it up."

"Thanks. I'd better go. I'm at the Save-A-Buck."

"All right. I'll see you tomorrow at the funeral, and afterwards we'll finalize our plans for going to Dakota's."

We said our goodbyes, and I hurried to enlist the aid of two baggers who'd come outside to return carts to the store. With their help, I managed to fit all eight cakes into three carts.

The young men helped me push them inside before returning to their original task, and I discretely tipped them.

There was no one in Juanita's line, so she came over and helped me unload the cakes onto a display table near the front of the store.

"How are you?" I asked.

"I'm good. I took some food over to Mrs. Duncan before I came to work this morning."

"That was sweet of you."

"Do you know the funeral is tomorrow?" she asked.

"Yes," I said. "I'll be there. Will you get to go?"

She nodded. "I took the day off so I could be there for Mrs. Duncan and the rest of Fred's family."

"Hey, were you working here when Fred had his car accident last year?"

"No. I came to work here shortly after that time." She noticed someone approaching her register. "We'll talk more later."

I finished arranging the display, and then I went in search of Mr. Franklin to let him know I'd brought the cakes he'd requested. I found him in his office hunched over his desk.

"Daphne," he said, standing up behind his desk. "Come on in." His dress shirt was wrinkled and his tie was stained. I thought—not for the first time—that he needed a wife. He wouldn't be bad looking if he'd try to be a bit neater with his appearance.

"I've brought the cakes you requested. Juanita and I arranged them on the display table."

"Very good."

"Is there anything else you'll be needing within the next couple weeks?" I asked. "I'm trying to coordinate my holiday schedule."

"Ah." Mr. Franklin sat and indicated I should do the same. "Are Christmas wedding bells ringing for someone in Brea Ridge?"

"Not that I'm aware of," I said, taking a seat. "However, Belinda Fremont is planning an extravagant New Year's Eve party."

He raised his brows. "This soon after Guinevere's birthday party? That's odd."

"You mean, Belinda's New Year's Eve party isn't an annual affair?"

"No. The birthday party is normally the Fremont social event of the holiday season. There typically isn't another party until Spring."

"Does she throw birthday parties for all the guinea pigs?" I asked.

"Nope. Only Guinevere." He smiled. "You see, Guinevere's birthday coincides with Belinda's."

"So, in a way, she's actually throwing herself a party."

"In a way."

"Wonder why she decided to host a New Year's Eve party this year then?" I held up a hand. "Don't get me wrong; I'm glad she is, I just wonder what prompted it."

"Maybe it's something Richard wants."

Richard is Belinda's husband. He seems like a super nice guy—I met him briefly at Guinevere's birthday party when I brought the cakes. From what I understand, he travels extensively. Maybe Mr. Franklin was right. Maybe the party was for Richard.

"You could be right," I said. "Belinda mentioned his sister would be coming and that she's single again. Richard is hoping she'll meet someone."

"Maureen is single again?" Mr. Franklin asked. "She's . . . um . . . very sweet. I knew her way back when. Anyway, I'd be delighted if you could work the Save-A-Buck up some Christmas cookies, candies—maybe some fudge, peanut butter pinwheels, haystacks—things like that—some cupcakes and a few more cakes."

"All right, I'll see what I can do."

"Bring them in as you make them, and let me know what you've brought."

"Okay." I smiled, glad I'd anticipated this and bought some cookie and candy trays with lids during my trip to the chef's wholesale warehouse in Kingsport last week. "Will I see you tomorrow?"

At Mr. Franklin's frown, I added, "At the funeral."

"I'm afraid not, Ms. Martin. Several of my employees are taking the morning or the day off, and I'll be needed here. I did send over a pretty peace lily, though."

"That was nice."

Mr. Franklin nodded in agreement.

"You know, I was thinking about how you once told me Fred had changed after the car accident," I said.

"He did change. You can ask anyone."

"Oh, I believe you. But his cousin was filling me in about the accident the other day, and it made me wonder. Do you suppose some of Fred's anger wasn't the result of his brain injury but was caused by the fact that the driver who was at fault was never found and punished?"

Mr. Franklin's face had turned to flint. "Since I'm neither a brain surgeon nor a psychiatrist, I wouldn't know."

"No, of course not. None of us will ever know, will we?"

"No." His face softened slightly. "I hope he's at peace now."

## Chapter Six

The first thing I heard when I woke up the next morning was rain pelting the windows. When I was a little girl and it rained on a sad day, I thought all of Heaven was crying with me. Of course, I'm older and wiser now. And I know that some of the saddest days are some of the sunniest. Remember what a clear, gorgeous morning September 11, 2001 started out being?

I sighed and rolled over, clutching my pillow. Outside the rain continued beating against the house. I squeezed my eyes shut and came to the only logical conclusion: sometimes Heaven weeps with us and for us; and at other times, Heaven is simply all cried out.

I didn't want to get out of bed . . . didn't want to go out in the rain and drive to a church on the other side of town to comfort a widow who was burying her only child. I wanted to wake up . . . have this whole thing be a horrible nightmare. I wanted to relay the entire convoluted dream to Myra and have her ask what I ate before going to bed.

I held the pillow a little tighter, whispered a prayer for Connie, and then I tossed aside the pillow and got out of bed. I ambled to the kitchen and put a dark roast coffee pod into my single-cup coffee maker. I put a cup underneath the spout and emptied two packets of sweetener into it before the coffee began to brew.

As soon as the coffee was done, I took it and a chocolate almond biscotti into the living room and curled up on the sofa. I didn't turn the television on. I already had all the bad news I could handle this morning.

I was dipping the biscotti into the coffee when the phone rang. I started not to answer it for the very reason that I was dipping my biscotti into my coffee. I mean, here I am getting ready to put this much-anticipated morsel of biscotti into my mouth, and someone has the nerve to call and interrupt?

It rang again, and I ever so begrudgingly answered.

"Good morning," Violet said, as chipper as a songbird on the first day of spring. "Sorry to call so early, but I wanted to talk with you before the kids get up."

"Okay." Since it was Violet, I went ahead and bit my biscotti.

"What was that? Did you break a tooth on the phone or something?"

"I'm eating breakfast?"

"What are you having? Rocks?"

"Biscotti. And it's wonderful."

"Oh. Well, what about the game? Do you like it? Is it age appropriate?"

"Apparently, it's appropriate for all ages. I'm enjoying it, Myra is enjoying it, and I think Lucas will enjoy it, too. Leslie, too, for that matter."

"Did you say *Myra?*"

"Yeah. I had to rent another controller so we can both play at once."

"*Myra Jenkins?* You cannot be serious."

"I'm serious. Come over this afternoon and see for yourself." I dipped the biscotti back into the coffee.

"All right. I'll come over after lunch."

"Can you make it about one o'clock? I'm going to Fred's funeral at eleven-thirty this morning."

"That is this morning, isn't it? I sent flowers. I know I should probably go, but Jason and I are taking the children to early church and—"

"It's fine," I said. "Nobody said you have to go." I bit the biscotti. It really was good.

"I know. I just . . . . Well, you're going."

"I was there when he died, remember?"

"Oh. Yeah. Oh."

"So, let's hang up so I can enjoy my breakfast, and I'll look forward to seeing you at around one o'clock."

"Gotcha. Love you. Bye."

And with that, she was gone. That's one thing about

Violet. Absolve her guilt or feelings of impropriety, and she'll happily go along with whatever you say. It's probably a good thing she's not Catholic.

*

I arrived at the church at a quarter past eleven. It was already packed. I was somewhat surprised that Uncle Hal and Aunt Nancy had driven all the way from Roanoke to be here. Then I remembered that Uncle Hal and Walt Duncan, Fred's grandfather, were hunting buddies and had been for as long as I could remember.

I squeezed into the pew beside my bear of an uncle and kissed him on the cheek.

He smiled. "Hey, there, girl." His white hair and bright blue eyes reminded me so much of Dad.

Aunt Nancy, lean and elegant in her brown tweed suit, leaned across Uncle Hal to pat my hand. "Hi, sweetie. Nice of you to be here."

I smiled slightly, thinking that even though I'm forty, older relatives still treat me as if I'm in high school. It was like, "Hey, look at Daphne. She did the mature thing by coming to a funeral. What a good girl." I decided not to let it bother me and instead be grateful someone still thought of me as being young.

I scanned the rows of pews. I saw Connie, Fran, Carol and Mr. Duncan sitting on the front pew, along with a few other people I didn't know. Juanita was a couple rows in front of me with a couple other people I recognized from the Save-A-Buck. I saw China York and Myra come in together and sit near the back. There was no sign of Ben, though. Maybe something had happened at work, and he wasn't going to be able to come after all.

Members of the church choir began singing "Standing On the Promises." Fran turned, scanned the crowd and smiled briefly when she spotted me. She turned back around to face the choir.

I nudged Uncle Hal and whispered an invitation for him and Aunt Nancy to come back to my house for lunch after the funeral.

He thanked me but said he and Aunt Nancy had "filled up at a Cracker Barrel at about ten-thirty." He promised they'd be back to see me soon.

I understood. Uncle Hal didn't like to linger after emotional events.

In one way—the literal passing of time—the funeral seemed to be mercifully short. In another way—watching Fred's family and friends weep into tissues and handkerchiefs—the service seemed to last for hours. Upon concluding the funeral, the preacher invited the congregation to join the family at the Brea Ridge Mausoleum for interment.

The pall bearers solemnly stood and took their places around the casket. They slowly carried Fred down the aisle and out the front doors. The family followed.

I wanted desperately to go home. I was obligated to speak with Carol about having Fran help me with Belinda's party, but this was neither the time nor the place. I'd leave Carol a phone message after I got home.

Uncle Hal, Aunt Nancy and I walked to the vestibule. I hugged them goodbye and extracted another promise they'd come to visit me soon.

Ben was standing to the right of the double doors looking angry. I concluded this wasn't the ideal time to introduce him to my aunt and uncle, so I waited until they'd gone on to the parking lot before approaching Ben.

"Is everything okay?" I asked. I knew it was a stupid question, but I didn't want him to realize what bad vibes he was sending out.

"Your friend Cara Logan got here about the same time I did," he said. "I didn't even make it into the sanctuary because I was out here preventing her from taking photos of the casket and the grieving mother."

I merely stood there gaping.

"She finally left when I called 9-1-1. Threats weren't enough for her. I actually had to make the call."

I was still speechless. Ben placed his hand at the small of

my back and escorted me to the parking lot.

"I . . . I'm sorry," I said at last. "I had no idea Cara could be that heartless."

"Well, she can."

"I wonder if Dr. Holloway has seen that side of her?"

"Who knows? Who cares? I just want to put this whole fiasco out of my mind." He shook his head as if he were truly shaking the thought from his mind. "Pick you up at five o'clock?"

I smiled. "That'll be great. Thank you."

He kissed my cheek and strode toward his white Jeep. I could tell by his walk that he hadn't fully succeeded in putting Cara's callous behavior out of his mind.

I got in the Mini Cooper and cranked the heat. That rain was cold. It made me think of Sparrow and how much I needed to convince her to trust me and come inside the house.

*

As soon as I got home, I called and left a message on Fran and Carol's answering machine. "Good afternoon, Carol. This is Daphne Martin. I realize this isn't a good time, but I've been hired to cater a party for Belinda Fremont. If Fran is willing to learn, and if you're willing to grant her permission, I'd love to have her help. It would be a sort of paid apprenticeship. If Fran is interested, please let me know."

I hung up the phone and went to the bedroom to change clothes. It was a jeans, sweatshirt and wooly socks kind of day . . . until four o'clock anyway. I padded back into the kitchen and popped a couple slices of bread into the toaster. I got a salad plate, the orange marmalade and a knife and then stood in front of the toaster waiting for the toast to get done. And, yes, I sometimes think the microwave takes too long also.

After several seconds—or probably minutes even—the toast was done. I spread marmalade on each slice and sat down at the kitchen table to eat.

What nerve Cara had, coming to the funeral and attempting to get photos of Fred's mother.

The thought stopped me immediately. I dropped my toast

back onto the plate and grabbed the phone.

"Ben," I said when he answered the phone, "what about the mausoleum? Do you think Cara went there to get her photographs?"

"More than likely. But I'd already let Officer McAfee know what was going on, and he was keeping an eye on her."

I expelled a breath. "Thank goodness. I'm so glad you'd already thought of that."

"I was way ahead of you on that one."

We said our goodbyes. I was just finishing my toast when Violet came to the door.

She gave a perfunctory tap before coming on in. "Hi. What's up?"

"Cleaning up my lunch mess," I said, putting my plate in the dishwasher.

"Hmm. I wish meal cleanup was that easy for me."

"Would you like some toast and marmalade?"

"No, thanks. We stopped for lunch on the way home from church." She looked down at my feet and giggled. "Love your socks. Leslie would say you have Who feet . . . you know, the Who's from *The Grinch Who Stole Christmas?*"

I wriggled my toes. "You can call me Cindy Lou. Come take a look at this guitar game."

Violet followed me into the living room. I opened the armoire that housed my television and turned on the game. While waiting for it to boot up, I took the guitar controllers out of the coat closet.

"Are you ready to rock?" I asked, handing Violet a guitar.

"I guess so."

I rolled my eyes. "Myra was much more enthusiastic than you, and she's nearly twice your age. Get with the program."

"All right, all right. Show me what to do."

I started the tutorial for her, but she remained blasé.

"Okay," I said. "You're ready for a song." I turned on the dual controls and brought up my alter-ego Jessie.

"She's a little trashy, isn't she?" Violet asked.

"A little," I admitted, "but the kids probably see people

like her—even on cartoons—all the time on TV and the media. I mean, have you seen the Justice League's latest incarnation of Wonder Woman? Even Linda Carter never looked that good."

"I guess you've got a point."

I scrolled to Myra's character, Lizzie Bourdain. "This is Myra's gal."

"She looks downright scary." Violet tried to appear stern, but burst into giggles.

"Come on," I said. "Pick a character, and let's get started. I won't try to influence you either way. You can make up your own mind about whether or not the game is appropriate for Lucas and Leslie."

"Deal."

She chose a character who reminded me of Japanese animé. The woman was dressed in an outlandish purple outfit; but unlike most of the other female characters, her body was completely covered from neck to toe. She even had fuchsia elbow-length gloves. Her hair was long and pink with streaks of white. Her name? Sumi.

I put the game in beginner mode—Myra and I had already progressed to "medium"—and started the song, "I Love Rock-N-Roll." Sumi and Jessie began to play.

Violet was hesitant at first, but then she began to hit her stride. By the time the song had ended, she was ready to play it again.

"I think I can do better this time," she said. "Hit 'replay' or whatever you do to start it back."

"Same song?" I asked.

"Of course. We want to be able to do this one well before we move on to the next one."

And so we played "I Love Rock-N-Roll" five times. By the fourth run-through, Violet had us not only playing the song but singing it as well.

After the fifth rendition, Violet looked at the clock and gasped. It was three-thirty.

"I should've been back at home an hour ago," she said.

"What's your verdict of the game?"

"Even though the lyrics to some of the songs may be a bit questionable, Jason and I have instilled strong values in Lucas and Leslie. They know right from wrong. I believe they'll have fun with this game." She grinned. "As a matter of fact, I think we all will."

\*

For my date with Ben, I wore a red jersey wrap dress and black velvet heels. I pulled my hair back from my face and secured it with a silver clip. I wore silver hoop earrings to match the hair clip.

When Ben came to pick me up, he handed me a manila envelope. "Copies of the articles you wanted."

As I started to open the envelope, Ben took it back and placed it on the counter. "Later," he said. "I've got reservations."

I frowned. "Since when does Dakota's require reservations?"

"They don't. But I've got reservations about your opening that envelope. I would like to go to dinner sometime this evening."

"Okay. It can wait."

"Thank you. By the way, you look incredible."

"Thanks. You clean up well yourself."

He looked fantastic. He was wearing a white shirt, khakis and a navy sport coat. He sort of looked like a newscaster . . . a really handsome newscaster. I'd tune in.

As we walked into the restaurant, I felt happy. I was optimistic we were going to have a delightful evening. That feeling lasted until after the waitress had brought our drinks and taken our meal orders. It was when she was walking away that my warm fuzzy feelings dissipated. That's when I looked up and spotted Cara Logan and a man who could be none other than John Holloway approaching our table.

## Chapter Seven

"What--?" Ben didn't have the chance to finish his question.

"Hi!" Cara smiled broadly. "John, I'd like you to meet Daphne Martin. Or have you two met already?"

"No, I haven't had the pleasure." Dr. Holloway, a short, thin man with a round face and round glasses, shook my hand.

"Oh. I thought you might've met Daphne since she catered your holiday party," Cara said.

"No, darling. Dr. Broadstreet handled the planning of that event."

"Besides," I said, "I was only responsible for the cake."

Cara turned to Ben and squeezed his hand. "John, I do believe you've met Brea Ridge's local newspaper reporter. I didn't know he and Daphne were an item, though." She wagged her finger at me as if I'd been a naughty girl.

"Yes, I've met Mr. Jacobs," Dr. Holloway said. "Good to see you again."

Ben nodded. His jaw muscles were clenching, cluing me—and, unless Cara and Dr. Holloway were only semi-conscious, them—that he was grinding his teeth.

Obviously, Cara was indeed only semi-conscious because the next words out of her mouth were, "Mind if we join you?"

I did not utter a sound. I simply sat and looked at Ben.

"Darling, I think perhaps we're intruding," Dr. Holloway said.

"Aw, come on," Cara said, swishing her hair off her shoulders. "You're not still miffed at me for my intrusion earlier today, are you, Benny?"

"Intrusion?" Dr. Holloway asked.

"Yes. It appears Benny here thought I was trying to steal his story this morning," Cara said. "I tried to explain he and I are working different angles and venues, but I don't think I ever quite persuaded him."

Ben finally turned his glare upon Cara. "Trying to photograph a grief-stricken mother at her son's funeral is reprehensible, no matter what angle or for what venue you're working, Ms. Logan."

"Cara?" Dr. Holloway looked to his companion for an explanation.

"Oh, John, I wasn't hiding in the bushes or anything. I merely thought my readers would appreciate a visual to help them understand the community's sense of loss over this young man's death."

Dr. Holloway nodded as if that made perfect sense. And, of course, the way Cara was spinning it, it almost did.

"But what about Brea Ridge Pharmaceuticals?" I asked. "Won't reader sympathy toward Fred and his family reflect badly on them . . . make the company and its doctors out to be villains?"

"Excellent point," Cara said. "Here's why it won't. Mr. Duncan was a medical anomaly. For some reason, the drug that practically saved the lives of numerous others failed to be effective in this one isolated case." She smiled and wrapped her arms around John. "That's the medical mystery my article will solve. And, as for the BRP doctors, they're heroes . . . particularly John."

Dr. Holloway blushed and gave Cara an "aw-shucks-golly-gee" look.

"Excuse me." Ben got up and made a beeline for the restroom.

I smiled stiffly at Cara and Dr. Holloway. I realized the polite thing for me to do would be to invite them to sit down, but I was afraid that doing so might make Ben's head explode.

"Daphne, it was a pleasure meeting you, but I believe Cara and I should hail that hostess and get a table before the restaurant becomes too crowded."

I smiled. "Of course. It was nice to meet you, too, Dr. Holloway."

"Say our goodbyes to Benny for us, won't you?" Cara asked.

"I will."

Benny. Ben had always hated being called that. Benjamin was acceptable. He'd even answered to BJ for awhile in high school. But never "Benny." Cara seemed to be a pro at pushing people's buttons.

They departed and easily located the hostess. She was at the front of the restaurant at her usual post.

As she was leading Cara and Dr. Holloway to an available table, Cara turned and waved to me over her shoulder. I was saved from returning the gesture by the waitress bringing our food.

Ben returned, said he wasn't feeling well and asked if we could get our food put in to-go boxes and leave. Naturally, I said yes. He signaled the waitress and asked for the check and the boxes.

Within minutes, Ben was dropping me of at my house. I asked if he'd like to come in.

"I can reheat our meals, and we can eat in the kitchen . . . just the two of us," I said. "I'll even light a candle."

"No, thanks, Daphne. I really do need to go on home."

"Okay. I hope you get to feeling better." I was thinking that maybe if he didn't get to feeling better, Dr. Holloway might have something that would fix him right up; but I knew way better than to express that thought. As things now stood, I didn't know if Ben was genuinely ill or if he was merely angry with me. For what, I couldn't fathom . . . unless it was the simple fact I had the audacity to be acquainted with Cara Logan.

With my to-go box in one hand, my key in the other and my black velvet wristlet hanging from my arm, I made my way to my side door. It's the one just off the driveway which opens into the kitchen, and it's the one I use most often.

As I put the key in the lock, I heard Sparrow meow. Even though she had food in her bowl, the smell of my dinner had drawn her out. She brushed against my leg.

I opened the door and turned on the kitchen light. "Come on, Sparrow. Let's go in." I stepped into the kitchen and held the door open. "Come on."

I stiffened in anticipation as she cautiously but daintily eased up onto the step to peer into the kitchen. She looked up at me and back to the interior of the kitchen. She put one white-tipped paw into the kitchen before turning and leaping off the step.

Since she'd made such a valiant effort, I opened my to-go box, tore off a piece of my chicken breast and put it in Shadow's bowl. She certainly didn't hesitate before pouncing on that.

I transferred my food to a plate and heated it in the microwave. While the food was heating, I went into the bedroom and changed into my pajamas.

I returned to the kitchen, removed my plate from the microwave and placed it on the kitchen table. I poured myself half a glass of white wine and even lit a couple votive candles. I didn't need Ben to have ambience and enjoy my unevenly reheated meal.

I got a napkin, knife and fork; and, while I was at it, I snagged the envelope Ben had brought earlier. Before I sat down, I put on a classical music CD to play softly. Did I mention I was determined to have some stupid ambience?

I sat down, took a sip of my wine and tasted the chicken. It wasn't bad. It would probably have been much tastier when it was first served, but even being cold and reheated hadn't ruined it.

I removed the articles from the envelope.

*At approximately five-thirty yesterday afternoon, a two-car accident on Fox Hollow Road left nineteen-year-old Fred Duncan in serious condition. Mr. Duncan swerved to miss a car that had crossed over into his lane. He then struck a utility pole.*

*An eyewitness had seen a car weaving from lane to lane on Fox Hollow Road mere minutes prior to the accident and had phoned the police. The eyewitness, Donald Harper of 301 Fox Hollow Road, had arrived at his home and exited his vehicle when he heard the crash. Harper, a certified paramedic, had his wife call 9-1-1 as he raced to the scene. Prior to the arrival of police and ambulance personnel, Harper administered first aid to the victim.*

*Neither Harper nor Duncan was able to get the other driver's license tag number. The vehicle has been described as a black, four-door BMW sedan. Police are seeking the driver, who fled the scene. Anyone with information regarding this case is asked to please contact the Brea Ridge Police Department.*

The second article featured an interview with Fred and a follow-up on his condition. First there was a recap of the accident and another plea for anyone with information to come forward.

*When asked what he recalls about the accident, Fred Duncan responds, "Not much. I was running an errand for Mr. Franklin, my boss at the Save-A-Buck. All of a sudden, I saw a black car coming right at me. I jerked the wheel to the right. I don't remember anything after that."*

*Mr. Duncan remains in guarded condition at Brea Ridge Memorial Hospital with a head injury.*

Harper. Donald Harper. I'd look up his phone number tomorrow. While I was at it, I made a mental note to ask Mr. Franklin what kind of errand Fred was running when he had the accident.

I finished eating and blew out my candles. I refrained from making a wish. I was stuffed, but I still managed to straighten the kitchen up before going into the living room to relax. I opened the armoire and got the TV remote. I stretched out on the sofa and cuddled up in a plush blanket as I began to channel surf.

The phone rang, and I muted the television before answering. I didn't go into the "Daphne's Delectable Cakes" spiel because most of my cake customers call during the day.

"Hello, Ms. Martin. This is Carol Duncan. Fran wants to help you cater Mrs. Fremont's party, and I'm willing to help out, too."

Was this the same Carol Duncan who'd had breakfast here Friday morning? The same Carol Duncan who'd shot laser beams out her eyes at me the entire time she was here?

I took so long to respond, she thought I'd hung up.

"Ms. Martin?" she asked.

"Um . . . yes, Mrs. Duncan, I'm still here. But I'm afraid I can't afford to pay very much for this catering help. That's why I was hoping to hire a high school student. You know, I could pay a nominal fee, and the student could gain knowledge of baking and catering, get some work experience and have an employment reference later on."

"Oh, I understand your position, but I'll work for free."

"I couldn't possibly ask you to do that," I said.

"Nonsense. I know my way around a kitchen right well. I believe I could be a valuable asset to you in making sure this party is successful."

"I'm sure you could, Mrs. Duncan, but I honestly can't afford to pay you."

"I've already told you I'd do it for nothing."

"But why would you do that? It's a lot of work."

"B-because." Mrs. Duncan cleared her throat. "Because I've always wanted to see inside that big house."

\*

I got up at around seven o'clock the next morning, had a cup of coffee and a biscotti (I really need to lay off those things, but they are so good), and got dressed. Myra had called last night after I'd hung up from talking with Carol Duncan. She'd learned at Tanya's Tress Tamers that there was, in fact, a medical research facility in Haysi. So, going on what we knew—that there was a medical research facility and a great little fabric shop in Haysi—we decided a road trip was in order to determine why Fred might have been going there so often. From what I could see of his room, he wasn't big into sewing.

I put on jeans, a white mock turtleneck, a green wool blazer and a pair of black ankle boots. Should the car break down, I didn't want to be underdressed for a trek in the country near "the Grand Canyon of the South," which is also known as Breaks Interstate Park. It's a beautiful place but, man, is it rugged. At least, it looked rugged in the pictures I'd seen. And I don't do rugged terribly well . . . especially in the winter. In fact, I was packing a blanket and some granola bars into the back of the Mini Cooper when Myra arrived.

"We are coming back today, aren't we?" she asked.

"Yes. This is just in case something happens."

She looked into the back of the car and cocked her head. "Like what? A rock slide?"

"I hadn't even considered a rock slide. You don't suppose . . . ?"

"No, I don't," she said. "Sorry I mentioned it. Everything will be fine. Even if there was a rock slide—which there won't be—surely someone would find us before we could eat twenty-four granola bars. Don't you think?"

"Myra, 'better safe than sorry' is a cliché, but it's a cliché for a reason."

She nodded. "Yeah. I think I've heard you say that a time or two before." She smiled. "Are we all set then?"

"I just need to feed the cat before we go."

I stepped back into the kitchen and got the bag of dry cat food. I filled Sparrow's bowl and then set an additional butter bowl full of food on the porch, too.

Myra arched a brow. "In case we don't get back?"

"Exactly. Violet's first thought might not be to check on the cat."

"Good thinking. Well, since you've got all the bases covered, shall we go? Do I need to sign a waiver or something first?"

I pressed my lips together. "You think I'm neurotic, don't you?"

"Only in a good way." She patted my arm. "I think it's nice that you're so thoughtful and cautious. Martha Stewart would be proud."

We got into the car, and I backed out of the driveway. "Since the drive there is a little over an hour, I found us an abridged book on tape to listen to," I said. It's an Agatha Christie mystery."

"See? You do think of everything. However, I'd like to chat awhile first, especially since I'm not sure I want to have thoughts of being buried at the Breaks with John Swift's silver running through my head if we do, in fact, encounter a rock slide."

"John Swift's silver? You mean, Jonathan Swift, the writer?"

"No, I don't mean Jonathan Swift, the writer. I mean John Swift, the ship captain." Myra settled back in her seat, and her voice took on that once-upon-a-time timbre favored by storytellers the world over.

"Legend has it," Myra said, "that John Swift left the sea for a life of trading among the Cherokee. Sometime after the French and Indian war, old Johnny met up with a man by the name of George Munday. Now Munday was a Frenchman taken prisoner during the war, and he spoke the languages of several Indian tribes. Munday told our Johnny about a rich silver vein in the wilderness."

"The wilderness?"

"Have you ever seen Breaks Interstate Park?" she asked.

"Only in pictures."

"It's pretty wild. Back to my story. This Munday fellow told John Swift that he and his family were mining the silver when a band of Shawnee attacked and killed Munday's father and brothers. I reckon because he could speak their language, they kept Munday and made him a slave to work in their silver mines in Kentucky.

"Munday talked John into going back with him to find the mine. The legend speaks of a journal John kept recording all their adventures. They found the silver and mined it for years. Then the American Revolution broke out, and the British put poor, old John in prison. By the time he got out, he was old and blind and didn't know where the silver was anymore."

"So why is his treasure believed to be at Breaks Interstate Park?" I asked.

"I don't know. It's as good a place as any, I reckon."

"Well, that was a let down."

"Want me to make something up?"

"Yes, especially since you won't let me listen to my book."

"Fine. You know about Paul Revere and that bunch in

Boston that had a lookout for the British? Well, they weren't the only ones. Minutemen everywhere were at the ready. Since John was English but had American sympathies, he figured that wouldn't go over well with the British army. So, he began to grab up bags of silver in hopes of hiding it and laying low until after the war. See, he'd met himself a little woman, and they'd built a little cabin, and they were all fixed up to get married and live a little-house-on-the-prairie life.

"Well, wouldn't you know it, John made one too many trips to the mines after bags of silver. He got caught. The British confiscated that last bag of silver and threw poor John in prison. His little woman tried to visit, but he sent her away."

Myra placed a hand on her chest. "'Go away from me, my dear Mary,' he told her. 'You must not see me like this. Live in our little cabin, and I will come to you anon . . . after these red coats let me out of prison.'"

"Anon?" I asked.

"Yes, anon. Would you let me tell my blasted story?"

"Yes. Please continue."

"But the British didn't release John until he was old and blind and pitiful. And poor Mary was even more pitiful because she'd had to keep up the little log cabin and forage for food and wash her clothes in the creek and all that jazz without her man or any electricity. She probably even had to chop wood, for goodness sake! The end."

"The end? Didn't John ever make his way back to her?"

"No, he was blind and didn't have directions. Besides, she had all she could handle taking care of the wood chopping and cleaning and scrounging for food and cooking the food and mending her clothes. She didn't have time to take care of an old, blind man. Give her a break already." She thought a second. "And that's why they call it the Breaks Interstate Park. There. *Now* the end."

"You still didn't tell me why people think the money is buried there."

She sighed. "Because that's where Mary's cabin was. Happy?"

"No. If all the silver was there, wouldn't she have known it and used it to have a better life?"

"Good grief. Is there no pleasing you? First, she was waiting for John to come back. By the time she realized he wasn't coming, she'd forgotten where the silver was. Besides, no amount of money would've given her a better life because she couldn't have used it to buy the stuff that would have made her life better because it had not been invented yet—electricity, dishwasher, washing machine, dryer. I know they try to romanticize all that olden days junk on television, but that's a lot of hooey. Times were hard. People worked from daylight to dark and probably had callused calluses. No, thanks."

I laughed. "Sewing by candlelight is not for you then?"

"No, ma'am. I like my modern conveniences, thank you. And two of my favorites are electric lighting and sewing machines. Now, are we there yet, because I'm storied out."

\*

By the time we did get to Haysi, the narrator for Agatha Christie's book had put Myra to sleep. She was snoring softly. I pulled into a parking space near the fabric shop. I thought maybe someone there or someone on the street could give us directions to the medical research facility.

I gently touched Myra's shoulder.

"What?!" she yelled, straightening up and looking about wildly.

"It's okay," I said with a grin. "We're here."

"Oh . . . yeah. I know. I was just . . . ."

"Resting your eyes?"

"That's it."

We went into the fabric shop. It was cool in the shop, as if it lacked adequate heating. The proprietor was sitting in a rocking chair by the window with a space heater at her side and a long green . . . something . . . she was crocheting. For some reason, the heavy woman with her squinting black eyes and her gray hair pulled into a bun reminded me of Madame Defarge. That was ridiculous, of course; Madame Defarge was a knitter, not a crocheter.

"Help you?" Madame said, barely glancing up from her work.

"We're just looking," Myra said. "I haven't been here in years, but I remembered you have a great little shop here."

"Thank you. But it's not my shop. It's my sister's. I'm watching it today while she does some Christmas shopping."

"Well, I'll just browse around then," Myra said.

"Help yourself."

I inched closer, wondering if you could actually crochet names into a long piece of green whatever. If you could knit names into something, you could surely crochet names into it.

"Help you?" the woman asked.

"I was just admiring your work," I said. "I can't crochet."

She nodded and looked back down at her work. She never dropped a stitch, and I thought that probably meant she was pretty good.

"Somebody told us there's a medical research place near here," I said. "Do you know where it might be?"

This actually made Madame stop crocheting. "What do you want to go there for? Ya'll don't look hard up to me."

"Hard up?" I asked.

"Yeah. Ain't you going there to volunteer to be a guinea pig? I hear the pay is fairly decent, but ain't no way I'm gonna volunteer to test drugs. Too many people have had bad experiences there." She shook her head. "They're doing some weird stuff over there, I'm telling you. They take advantage of people that's fell on hard times. I've seen people get worse. But I ain't ever seen anybody get better from going there."

## Chapter Eight

After what Madame Defarge had said about the medical research facility, I was afraid there would be junkies and all sorts of scary looking people lurking outside. There was, in fact, no one outside—lurking or otherwise. Unless they were lurking in the bushes. We didn't see a soul.

Myra and I walked in to the sterile looking facility, which appeared much like any other doctor's office. Black chairs lined the walls, broken up in twos and threes by wooden tables piled with outdated magazines. At the moment, all the chairs were empty. To the left was a receptionist's window, enclosed by a glass partition.

I stepped up to the receptionist's window. The receptionist—a woman with short red hair and glasses with tortoise shell frames—looked up and opened the window.

"Hello," she said. "Do you have an appointment?"

"No, we're here to ask about someone who might have been a patient here."

"We're not allowed to give out any information on test subjects," she said.

"Well, I'm not even sure he *was* a test subject. His name is Fred Duncan. Can you tell me if he's on your client list?" I asked.

"No, I can't. We're bound by strict confidentiality agreements with both our test subjects and our corporate sponsors." She closed the window.

"Well, she has a nerve," Myra said.

I knocked on the glass. "Is there someone else I can speak with?"

The receptionist shook her head. "No. If you don't leave now, I'll be forced to call the police department."

Myra and I left. She had bought lots of cute fabric at Madame Defarge's shop, but I doubted they'd let her do anything with it in jail.

"This bugs me," I said, as we left. "Let's find a library and see if we can't dig up more on this medical research/test subject stuff. Maybe we can find something that will make her tell us whether or not Fred was working for them."

"You go ahead. I'll thumb through some magazines. I'm not dealing with her and her nasty little threats anymore."

The library wasn't hard to find. I was relieved to discover that it was comfortable and had a friendly staff, especially since the earlier two receptions I'd received in this town were about as warm as an ice chest.

"Hi, there," said a tall, thin woman with a dark blonde, shoulder-length bob. "May I help you find anything?"

"Do you have computers for public use?" I asked.

"We sure do. Do you have a library card with us?"

"I'm afraid not. I'm from Brea Ridge and I'm here on business."

"You got a Brea Ridge library card?" she asked.

"Yes."

"Well, that's good enough for me." Smiling, she led me to the public computers and signed me in. "Let me know if you need anything."

I did a search for human test subjects and clinical drug trials, and I learned quite a bit. One article spoke about researchers' lack of upfront information to test subjects, indicating they weren't informed about the unknown problems scientists are paying "guinea pigs" to find. Another article mentioned that some researchers refuse to share information about the number of human test subjects they employ, the types of studies they perform or how many adverse reactions have occurred during their studies.

The most recent article—one which appeared in *Wired Magazine, Issue 15.05*—discussed the disturbing trend of some "guinea pigs" to make a career of being a test subject. The article also indicated the existence of such inane studies as "the impact of the club drug GHB on driving ability."

"You've got to be kidding me."

I didn't realize I'd spoken the thought aloud until the

librarian asked, "I'm sorry. Did you say something?"

"Oh . . . um . . . I came across an article on human research test subjects. Don't you guys have a medical research facility near here?"

"We do."

"And does that facility use human test subjects?"

"I believe so."

"What do you think about it?" I asked.

"About humans volunteering to be test subjects or the research facility being located in our town?"

"Both."

"Well, if somebody wants to be a test subject, I guess that's up to him or her. I'm sure the researchers explain the risks and the fact that they may or may not be on a drug. After all, you have to have the mean, right? Isn't that what they call it?"

"I don't know."

"Besides, I figure the people who allow themselves to be tested on know what they're doing. Personally, I wouldn't do it. But I've talked with people who have, and they act like it's no big deal. As far as the facility goes, it did bring in a few new jobs."

"Thanks."

"You're welcome."

I retrieved Myra from the pages of *Modern Woman*, and we headed home.

"So do you think Fred was coming over here to take part in some freaky Frankenstein experiments or something?" Myra asked.

"I don't know. If something shows up in the autopsy report that the coroner finds odd, then I suppose it's a possibility. But the librarian pointed out something I hadn't thought of with regard to the testing."

"What's that?"

"Even if Fred was coming over here and taking part in some sort of clinical trials, he wasn't necessarily being given the drug being tested. Some people are given a placebo so the doctors can observe the differences between the two groups."

"Hmm. I'd love to have a gazebo. Not this time of year, naturally, but during the late spring, summer and early fall, I think it'd be great."

I smiled. "Myra, you are priceless. What are you planning to do with all that fabric?"

"Oh, I have all sorts of plans. Tote bags, dresses, blouses, place mats, curtains. But, in truth, I'll probably put it in the sewing room with all the rest of my junk and forget I have it." She shrugged. "But at least I have pretty new fabric, and it'll be there if I take a notion to do something with it. If we have some snowy days, I'll probably get bored and decide to do something. Might even make you a new apron."

"Wow, I'd love it."

"Then you'd better pray for snow. And keep the baked goods coming."

"Hey, do you remember when Fred had his car accident?" I asked.

"Yep," Myra said with a nod. "Everybody in town was on the lookout for that car—and not just because it wrecked Fred, but because we were all afraid we'd be next. I mean, of course, we were all upset about what happened to Fred. He'd always been a good boy . . . never been in trouble. But the fact that whoever was driving that car didn't take responsibility for his—or her—actions . . . well, that bothered us all. Before that, we'd all felt like Brea Ridge was a town with integrity."

"That shook your faith, huh?"

"Yeah. I mean, you know there are bad apples in every tree, but it wasn't just the driver."

"What do you mean?"

"Well, somebody else had to know about that car wreck. I mean, if there was an accident where the driver pulled a hit and run, and the police were looking for a little red car, and you came home with your car all boogered up, I'd have to ask you about it."

"I know that's the truth," I said.

"But, let's say you came home at night and had a garage

and you hid the car in there, people would have to see it when you drove it again . . . unless you had somebody come to your garage to fix the car. And, in that case, the person who fixed your car would know."

"And what if I'd suffered an injury?"

"Exactly," Myra said. "And if you'd hit a car as hard as that one hit Fred's—"

"Wait a sec. I thought Fred hit a utility pole."

"He did, but that other car still clipped the back hard enough to crush the back end of Fred's car. Plus, the police found one of the other car's hubcaps in the road."

"So there was no question that the other car was damaged."

"Right."

I nodded slowly. "So now you've got a car that has to be fixed unless the driver has alternative means of transportation, a driver who might be hurt—not to mention drunk—and when you add all that together, you have at least a handful of people who have a decent suspicion of who the other driver was."

"Yep. There could be a mechanic. There could be a bartender or a liquor store clerk who knows someone with that type of car was drinking that afternoon." She shook her head. "Yet the police never got a single lead. That bothers me."

"It bothers me, too."

*

When we got home, I invited Myra in. We'd stopped in Lebanon for some lunch, but I thought she might want to come in for awhile. She didn't. She said she needed to get home and put her fabric away . . . "stuff like that" and that she'd talk with me later.

I was relieved. I love Myra to pieces, but I wanted to relax for awhile before Connie and Fran came over to discuss catering Belinda's party.

The first thing I did when I went in was check my messages. The answering machine was blinking like the dickens. Excited, I hit play.

The first message was from Violet. "Where are you today? Is everything okay? You didn't mention going Christmas shopping today, and it isn't like you to blow everything off—especially during this time of year—to take some unscheduled trip. Call me. I'm concerned."

*Yes, Mom.*

The second message was from Ben. "Hi. Still feeling lousy. I'll call you back later. Hope you're not sick."

The third message was from Cara. "Daphne, hi! It's Cara Logan. You guys disappeared on us last night. What happened? I hope I didn't upset Benny. Call me, okay?"

There was another message from Violet. "Hey, it's me again. I ran into Julie, who waits tables part-time at Dakotas. She said you and Ben were there last night and that either Ben got sick or you two had a fight and left. She wasn't sure which since she heard it both ways." Her voice softened. "I hope everything is all right. Call me when you can."

I rolled my eyes. *Great. Now she thinks Ben and I have had some major argument, and I'm holed up at home with my Ben & Jerry's crying and watching sappy movies.*

There was one last message, and it was from Uncle Hal. "Call me. I'm hearing unpleasant rumors about you . . . but don't say anything about that to your Aunt Nancy."

*Who am I? Daphne Jolie? Since when did I become the subject of unpleasant rumors, and when did people start speculating about Ben and me? Or should I call us Benphe? Or Daphen? Grrr. All those calls and not a single cake order. Double grrr.*

I returned Violet's calls first.

"Violet," I said when she answered. "Can you come get me? I'm trapped beneath a house in Oz."

"Oh, ha-ha; you're so funny . . . although I'd almost believe that considering the socks you were wearing yesterday. Where've you been all day? And if you say something stupid, I swear I'll hang up on you and call Mom."

"You're bluffing."

"Try me."

"I've been to Haysi with Myra."

"Because . . . ."

"Because she wanted to visit a fabric shop over there."

"You dropped everything during a peak baking season to take Myra to a fabric shop an hour and a half away? I don't think so."

"You can call and ask her yourself."

"I know there's more to it, and you'd better tell me right now before I call Mom."

"You will so not call Mom," I said. "Stop threatening me with that. Like the rest of us, you're still creeping around on eggshells with her out of fear she'll have another heart attack."

"Right, but what do you want to bet every odds maker on the Blue Ridge Parkway thinks something you do or say will be the very pain down the left arm that sends Mom back to the emergency room?"

"I cannot believe you just said that to me." And I really couldn't. Violet is the golden child. She'd never hurt Mom, even if it was to spite me. "Besides, whoever said there are odds makers on the Blue Ridge Parkway? That's ridiculous."

Violet sighed. "I'm sorry."

"What would you tell Mom anyway? That I took a neighbor shopping? Would that be such a complete shock to her as to cause a myocardial infarction?"

"No, I'd tell her the truth. I'd tell her you're investigating another death."

"Vi, look it—"

"No, you look. I care about you, and I don't want to see you put yourself in jeopardy again. Let it go."

"Okay."

"I've heard that before," Violet said. "I don't know what you're doing, and I doubt you do either, but I don't want to be around you—and I won't have my children around you—if you've got a target on your chest."

"I don't blame you. And, honestly, I'm through with this . . . pretty much."

"Pretty much."

"No, seriously, I'll tell Ben what little I know and let him and Cara Logan hash out the rest of it."

"Cara Logan. Why does that name sound familiar?"

"I met her in September at the Oklahoma Sugar Art Show in Tulsa."

"That's right. She works for a paper in Northern Virginia, doesn't she?"

"Yes, plus she's dating John Holloway of Brea Ridge Pharmaceuticals. She's in a much better position to investigate Fred's death than I am."

"You mean it?"

"I mean it. I've had enough drama . . . well, except for Belinda Fremont's New Year's Eve soiree."

Violet laughed. "Ooh, la, la. I suppose we're toasting the arrival of Cavy New Year."

"Something like that," I said with a giggle. "You know, Belinda would probably adore that concept."

"Well, good luck with that. I'd better get back to work before I have to fire myself."

"Oh, yes, being self-employed bites."

"It does when the market is as slow as it has been lately."

"Are you guys okay? I could use some help catering this party and—"

"We're fine, Daph. Jason's job is secure, and we're doing great. It's you I worry about."

"And it's you *I* worry about."

We shared another laugh and reassured each other that neither of us has anything to worry about before hanging up.

My next call was to Uncle Hal. Lucky for me—I guess—he answered on the first ring.

"Hey, Uncle Hal. It's me, Daphne. Is this a good time for you to talk?"

"Yeah, honey, this is a fine time. Your Aunt Nancy is visiting one of the neighbors. She took them over some Christmas candy."

"That was nice." I decided then I might as well dive in with both feet. "You said you've heard some unpleasant rumors."

I steeled myself for another lecture on investigating Fred Duncan's death and rehearsed my response. It was, of course, along the same lines of what I'd told Violet—which was the truth, I'm out of the detective business. I have a fancy-schmancy New Year's Eve party to work on.

I was so busy planning out what I wanted to say to Uncle Hal that when I didn't hear "Fred Duncan," I had to have him repeat himself.

"Is it true you've been running around with that newspaper fellow, Ben Jacobs?" he asked.

"We've had a few dates," I said. "I'm not sure that qualifies us as 'running around' together."

"I don't care what it qualifies as. All I know is that you'd better be awful careful with that man. He's dangerous."

# Chapter Nine

"What? Did you say Ben is dangerous?"

"You heard me."

"Do you know something I don't?"

"Obviously. Haven't you ever wondered why a nice-looking, successful man like Ben Jacobs has never married? Aren't you the least bit curious as to why he's not been in a serious relationship since his junior year of college?"

*Wow. And they call* me *an investigator. What was Uncle Hal . . . C.I.A.?*

"Please tell me you're not implying what I think you are," I said.

"You ought to know me well enough to realize I never imply anything. I come right out and tell it like it is. That man is a playboy, and he's gonna wind up breaking your heart. And I would hope you've had enough of that."

"Uncle Hal, I've known Ben since I was a little girl. He doesn't strike me as the playboy type."

"There's nobody so blind as the one who refuses to see."

"No, really. I think Ben hasn't been seriously involved with anyone because he's been focusing on his career . . . and taking care of his parents." I threw in that last part—albeit true—mainly to try and win Ben some brownie points with Uncle Hal. It didn't pay off.

"Is that what he's told you?"

"Yes . . . and I believe him. After all, if I'd spent my time focused on my career instead of in an abusive marriage, I might have my own bakery, or TV show or who-knows-what by now."

"Exactly. And yet, Mr. Jacobs is still right there in little old Brea Ridge."

"But, he likes it here. And he freelances for larger newspapers and magazines."

"Mm-hmm. Sounds to me like you need to spend more

time focused on your career and less time with manipulative jerks."

I sighed. When Uncle Hal gets like this, there's no reasoning with him. He's right, he knows what's best, you don't, end of discussion.

"All right, Uncle Hal. I'll be careful. Oh, by the way, how's Mr. Duncan doing?"

"As you can well imagine, he's torn all to pieces over Fred's death. That boy was his only grandson."

"I'm so sorry for that family," I said. "First to have Fred get hurt so badly in the car accident—with that hit-and-run driver never found and forced to face charges—and then this. It's tragic."

"It is that. I remember Walt Duncan turning that town inside out after Fred's car wreck looking for that other driver, the car or anybody who might know anything. To this day, Steve Franklin hurries to his office or to the storeroom—whichever's closest—anytime he sees Walt come into the Save-A-Buck."

"Why? Did Mr. Duncan think Mr. Franklin had something to do with Fred's accident?"

Uncle Hal snorted. "Franklin did have something to do with Fred's accident. He sent Fred out that rainy afternoon rather than running his errand himself like he should have."

"What errand?"

"To deliver flowers to Franklin's mother. It was her birthday."

"What? Why on earth would Mr. Franklin send one of his baggers to take his own mother a birthday gift instead of taking it himself?"

"Now that there is the million dollar question. He told Walt he was just too busy to leave the store. And yet, he had time to get a haircut earlier that day. Which brings me back to our original topic of discussion," Uncle Hal said. "No man is ever too busy or too focused on his career to do something he really wants to do. If he tells you otherwise, he's lying."

"I'll keep that in mind, Uncle Hal."

"You do that."

*

I called Ben and Cara. Both were apparently unavailable because both phone numbers went straight to voice mail. I left messages and then got ready to meet with Fran and Carol.

When they arrived, I had the kitchen set up in a Brigade system.

"Tonight we're doing cookies," I explained. "I don't advise tasting the cookie dough."

"Because of the raw eggs?" Fran asked.

"Because these are guinea pig cookies."

Both she and Carol made a face.

"They're probably not bad, just . . . ." I shrugged. "Vegetable and bland tasting, I imagine."

"We're only making enough cookies for Belinda's cavies to sample tonight. Then we're going to make some people cookies, candy and tarts. So, here's how this will work. I'll mix the ingredients into this bowl. Then I'll pass the bowl down the line to Carol, who will roll out the dough on the waxed paper. Carol will slide the waxed paper down to Fran who will use the water bottle cap beside the parchment-lined cookie sheets to cut guinea pig sized cookies and place them on the cookie sheets. The oven is already preheating and will be ready by the time the batch of cookies is done. Carol, if you don't mind, while Fran is cutting out the cookies, would you please put the bowl and spoon into the dishwasher? While you guys are taking care of those things, I'll be setting up the next assembly line."

"Sounds good to me," Carol said.

"Me, too," Fran said.

I put the ingredients into the bowl, mixed them up and slid the bowl to Carol. As I was putting away the cavy cookie ingredients, Carol flipped the dough onto the waxed paper, sprinkled it with flour and began rolling it out.

"What's she like? Mrs. Fremont, I mean," Carol said.

"She's nice," I said. "She wants things done a particular way; but once you and she have come to an agreement on that and she realizes you'll work your butt off to make things right for her, she's easy to work for. And, I have to say, she is awfully proud of that house."

"I can imagine." Carol slid the flattened dough down to Fran and took the bowl and spoon to the dishwasher. "What about the rolling pin?"

I tilted my head. "It hasn't had anything gross on it—just banana, honey, carrots and oats. Let's just wipe it off with a damp paper towel, okay?"

"Will do."

"Tell us about the house," Fran said, placing tiny cookies onto the baking sheet.

"In a word, wow," I said. "You know that saying, 'you had me at hello'? Well, the Fremonts had me at the driveway. It's a white and terra cotta mosaic. I always feel I should get out in the road and wash my tires before I drive up to the gate."

Fran and Carol laughed.

"You'll have to see it for yourselves." I grinned. "What are you guys doing tomorrow morning at eleven-thirty?"

"I have to work, but I can take my lunch break then," Carol said, her excitement evident in her voice.

"Good. Fran?"

"We're on Christmas break, so I'm at your disposal until after the first of the year."

"Great. Come with me to Mrs. Fremont's house."

Carol squealed like a little girl. I could not get over the change in her demeanor. It was as if her evil twin had been here the last time.

"What should I wear?" Carol asked.

"Something casual," I said. "Business casual. You don't want her to think you dressed up for her." I continued gathering the ingredients for pinwheels.

"I know, but it's almost like meeting the queen or something," Carol said.

I turned and held my whisk aloft. "I present to you Her Royal Highness Belinda Freemont, Queen of the Guinea Pigs."

"No, no," Fran said, with a giggle. "How about Countess Cavy?"

"Countess Cavy," I echoed. "I like it."

As we baked the cavy cookies and prepared the other samples, we discussed some of the other ideas Belinda had for the party and how Carol and Fran could help me pull off such a huge undertaking despite everything else going on within the next couple weeks.

I offered Carol and Fran a decaf café au lait, but they both declined.

"I appreciate it," Carol said, "but I'd better not. I need to get up early and go back to work tomorrow."

"Can we help you do anything else before we go?" Fran asked.

"No, but thank you for the offer. I'm going to make a couple batches of fudge to take to the Save-A-Buck tomorrow, but then I'm calling it a night myself." I got out my double boiler. "Speaking of the Save-A-Buck, do either of you know why Mr. Franklin sent Fred to his mother's house the day of Fred's car accident rather than going himself?"

"He—Mr. Franklin, I mean—told Papaw it was because his brother was visiting," Fran said.

"So? It was their mother's birthday," I said. "Lots of family members who don't get along suck it up and make nice for holidays and other events. What's so bad about Mr. Franklin's brother?"

Fran shrugged. "Dunno. Maybe he's a Cullen."

Carol rolled her eyes. "Again with the vampires? Honestly."

Catching their reference to the popular *Twilight* series, I said, "I'm more of a werewolf fan myself. That Jacob is adorable."

"Not you, too," Carol said. "I'll take Frannie and get out of here before you two start howling at the moon."

"New Moon," Fran and I said in unison. Then we exchanged high fives.

Carol shook her head. "I must be getting old."

I walked Fran and Carol to the door, turned on the porch light and waved goodbye as they backed out of the driveway.

The light had beckoned to Sparrow, so she eased out of hiding to investigate. I held the door open.

"Come on, Sparrow. Come inside and get a treat."

She gave me a look that plainly said, "What treat? I don't see any treat. Show me the treat, and maybe we'll pursue this further."

Doing some movements that would make your run-of-the-mill contortionist proud, I held the door open with my foot while turning and retrieving a can of tuna from the cabinet to my right. The can had a pull-top, so I opened it and sat it on the floor about eight inches—or a Sparrow length—from the door.

"How's that?" I asked. "Doesn't that smell good? Come on in and have a bite."

She looked as if she was trying to decide whether or not she was being tricked. I understood her hesitation. I've certainly fallen for my fair share of tricks.

For some reason, the conversation I'd had with Uncle Hal earlier sprang to mind. I shoved the thought aside and went back to concentrating on Sparrow.

"Come on," I said softly. "It's okay."

She eased closer to the step, but she still debated about trusting me.

Still holding the door open, I looked away from her. The detachment ploy worked. She quickly leapt onto the step and ran inside the kitchen. From the corner of my eye, I could see her turn back to me before risking a bite of the tuna.

I continued pretending to ignore her while holding the door open and praying I would not be besieged by moths, bugs, possums, raccoons, bats, owls, bears, coyotes, skunks . . . . I was running out of critters to be concerned about when Sparrow darted back outside.

I closed the door and turned out the porch light. I smiled and did a Tiger Woods' fist pump before tossing the empty tuna can into the trash and going to wash my hands.

*One small step for Sparrow; one giant leap for our relationship.*

When I returned to the kitchen, a large cricket was sitting

where the tuna can had been and was chirping for all it was worth.

"Did the Blue Fairy send you, Jiminy? Oh, well, it could've been worse, I suppose. You could've been a skunk."

\*

I'd just stepped my weary body out of the bathtub when the phone rang. I wrapped myself in my robe and hurried to the bedroom to answer it. It was Ben.

"How are you?" I asked.

"I think I'll live. I had my doubts up until earlier this evening."

"I'm glad you're feeling better."

"Yeah. Me, too. I don't think I would be if I hadn't received a call from Doc Holloway."

Visions of a tough but sickly Val Kilmer came to mind. No, wait, that was Doc Holliday. I shook off my musings as I leaned back against the pillows and asked, "Why did you get a call from him?"

"He was concerned because of the way I left the table last night. He said he didn't know if I was feeling ill or if I was merely upset at his and Cara's interruption. He told me that if it was the latter, he wanted to apologize. But I told him I'd become sick and still was. He asked me my symptoms, and I explained what was going on. Then he brought me over a dose of the vaccine he gave to the people at the Christmas party. I started feeling better within minutes."

"That's freaky. So does he think your illness was caused by the same bacteria?"

"He knows it was. He drove me to his clinic where he took some blood and tested it for that particular strain of bacteria. It was the same stuff."

"Then is Brea Ridge undergoing an epidemic?" I asked.

"Nobody knows . . . at least, not at this point. And, I'm asking you to keep this confidential. We don't want to cause a panic."

"No, of course, not. But other people need to know a vaccine is available if they do become sick."

"That's true," Ben said, "but I spoke with the manager of Dakota's. No one else who was there last night reported becoming ill. No one who works there has reported getting ill either. And, according to John, this bacterium is so aggressive, if it got on the food preparers' hands, they'd get sick, too."

"You hadn't even received your food before you got sick. Frankly, I thought you were upset about Cara and Dr. Holloway, too. Then, after you didn't come inside to finish having dinner with me, I thought you might be angry with me."

"Daphne, I told you I was sick."

"I know, but I thought you were simply saying that to avoid talking about what was really bothering you. That's what I'd do if I were trying to avoid a confrontation."

"Well, that's great. Now the next time you tell me you're not feeling well I'm going to wonder if it's because you're really not feeling well or because you're avoiding a confrontation. You have real trust issues, you know that?"

"Maybe a few. But, given my past, I'm entitled. Back to this bacterium—where does Dr. Holloway think you encountered this junk if it wasn't at Dakota's?"

"We don't know. On the one hand, John feels it would almost certainly have to have originated with me at Dakotas because I got so sick there. If you'll recall, the people at the Christmas party had a reaction within minutes of being infected."

"Did you eat or drink anything before you came to pick me up?"

"No, and John even asked me if I ate or drank anything at your house before we left for the restaurant."

"At my house?" I nearly shrieked. "But I haven't been sick. Don't tell me they're trying to tie this entire thing back to me and that stupid cake I took to that stupid party! That cake is being tested, and the police will see it was perfectly fine."

"Calm down. Nobody is blaming you for anything. I didn't eat or drink anything at your house before we left, remember?"

"Of course, I remember. I just . . . it's been a crazy day, that's all."

"Tell me about it."

"I'm sorry. I'm glad you're feeling better." After a rather awkward silence, I asked, "What if this is the start of an epidemic in Brea Ridge? Something has to be done before the children start back to school and especially before . . . ."

"Before other people wind up like Fred Duncan," Ben said.

"Exactly. So what do we do?"

"I don't know." Ben sighed. "As I said, Dr. Holloway doesn't want to create a panic. He wants people to think the bacteria incident was limited to the Christmas party . . . that it was just a fluke."

"Is that wise? I mean, obviously, the Christmas party was not an isolated incident or else you wouldn't have gotten sick from that same bacterium."

"I know, but what am I supposed to do? Print a story about it and scare everyone in town?"

I expelled a breath. "Yeah. That's a pickle."

"I'll sleep on it," Ben said. "Maybe things will look different in the morning."

Things definitely did look different the next morning. Cara Logan went on the local morning news show to warn people about the mysterious illness that is befalling the residents of Brea Ridge.

## Chapter Ten

I was roused from a peaceful slumber Tuesday morning by the shrill ring of the phone. Before I was fully awake, I thought it was the oven timer and tried to remember what I was baking. But then I remembered the oven timer was a continuous buzz, while this sound was intermittent. That's when the fog cleared, and I fumbled for the phone.

"Daphne's . . . Cake . . . Delicacies."

It was Ben. "Have you got your TV on?"

"I don't even have my brain on. What time is it? What's the matter?"

"Turn your TV on to Channel 2."

Fortunately, there's a small television on top of the chest of drawers in my bedroom. I was in no condition to be ambulatory. I propped up on my elbow and opened the drawer to my nightstand. Taking out the remote, I turned on the TV, put it on Channel 2, yawned and flopped back down in bed. The clock in the corner of the set told me it was 6:05 a.m. The station was showing a commercial for hemorrhoid cream.

I groaned. "Uh, I appreciate your concern, but I don't currently need this particular product. Or is this your roundabout way of telling me I'm a pain in your posterior?"

"What? No. It's coming up after the break."

"I have no idea what 'it' is; but unless a meteorite fell on the Save-A-Buck during the middle of the night or confectioner's sugar has been deemed an illegal substance, I'm not sure I care." I could suddenly see myself in a black trench coat meeting a seedy-looking character in a dark alley to buy a ten-pound bag of confectioner's sugar, dampening my ring finger and tasting the sugar to make sure it was "pure" before handing over the money.

*Mental note: Lay off the cop shows.*

"Oh, I think you'll be interested in this," Ben said.

"What time do you get up anyway?" I asked. "You do

realize it's barely six o'clock, don't you? The sun isn't even up."

"Shhh. Here it is."

Before I had time to go all indignant on him for calling and waking me up only to shush me, Cara appeared onscreen. She looked lovely in a gray pinstriped suit, pink blouse and gray spectator pumps. Wonder what time *she* got up this morning? I had to admit the girl was a natural for the news desk.

The anchorman was a Ken-looking type of guy—you know, Ken . . . as in Barbie and—whom I'd seen on the noon show a few times. He was saying something grave to the viewing audience. I turned up the volume to I could make out what he was saying.

"Cara, fill us in on this latest development."

"Thank you, Doug." The camera zoomed in on Cara. "As you mentioned earlier, we had all hoped—and indeed thought—the outbreak of an isolated strain of campylobacter which triggers intense gastrointestinal distress was limited to that suffered by those attending the Brea Ridge Pharmaceutical Christmas party several days ago. Unfortunately, another case has been reported."

The camera panned back out to include both Cara and Doug in the shot.

"And that has occurred here in Brea Ridge," Doug said.

"Precisely. Ben Jacobs, a reporter and editor for the *Brea Ridge Chronicle*, fell ill suddenly Sunday evening. When Dr. John Holloway of Brea Ridge Pharmaceuticals, learned of Mr. Jacobs' illness, he treated Mr. Jacobs with the same drug used successfully on ninety-nine percent of the people stricken by this strain of campylobacter at the aforementioned party. A blood test confirmed Jacobs had been infected with the same illness."

"Cara, after Fred Duncan's death following the administration of the experimental campylobacter drug, Campylophine, was there any hesitation on the part of Dr. Holloway or Mr. Jacobs in employing this remedy?"

"Not at all. It's apparent Mr. Duncan's death was an anomaly. There's currently nothing definitively linking his death to the drug. In fact, Dr. Holloway is encouraging anyone who shows symptoms of being affected by campylobacter to contact Brea Ridge Pharmaceuticals."

"A list of those symptoms will be displayed onscreen prior to our next break, and it will also be posted on our website," Doug said. "One last thing, Cara, do we know where Mr. Jacobs contracted the campylobacter?"

"We haven't a clue. However, no one else has shown symptoms. We're urging residents of Brea Ridge not to panic—we don't think there's any cause for alarm—but to simply remain vigilant."

"Again, that's Cara Logan of the *West Side Messenger* speaking with us this morning on behalf of Brea Ridge Pharmaceuticals. Thank you, Cara."

"My pleasure, Doug."

I'd almost forgotten Ben was still on the phone when he asked, "Can you believe that?"

*

I dropped four containers of chocolate fudge and four containers of peanut butter fudge off at Save-A-Buck as I drove to Carol's house to pick up her and Fran. I beeped the horn, and they quickly came outside.

Carol was looking nicer than I'd ever seen her. Her brown hair had been curled, she had on makeup, and she was wearing a royal blue wool suit and black knee-length boots.

Fran was wearing black pants, a white ruffled shirt and a teal blazer. She looked fresh and beautiful. But, then, she always does.

Fran allowed her mother to take the front seat, and she hopped in back with the baked goods.

"Carol, we'll make this as quick as possible," I said. "I don't want your lunch break to run too long."

"That's all right," she said. "Fran and I have already talked about that. If I go over my lunch hour, I'll stay after work to make it up; and she'll start dinner."

"Yeah, that way dinner will be ready when she and Dad get home," Fran said.

"Right. Pete will be late getting home tonight anyway," Carol said.

"Did he go back to work today, too?" I asked.

"No," Carol said. "He took an extra day to spend with his dad. They both needed it."

I nodded. "I spoke with my Uncle Hall the other day. He said Walt was taking Fred's death awfully hard."

"Pete is, too. Well, we all are, really," Carol said. "Fred was all we had left of Pete's brother Travis."

After that, we passed the couple remaining miles to Belinda's house in silence.

I pulled up to the gate, put down my window and pressed the intercom button. "Daphne Martin, Carol Duncan and Fran Duncan to see Mrs. Fremont please."

The anticipation emanating from Carol and Fran was nearly palpable.

"Come right in, Ms. Martin."

The gate slowly opened, and Fran and Carol gasped.

When we arrived at the house, we were shown into the parlor. Before Belinda joined us, however, Hilda the housekeeper came to get us. I introduced her to Carol and Fran.

"Mrs. Fremont has requested you meet with her in the dining room this morning, Ms. Martin. She said you may set up everything on the dining room table, and she'll join you in approximately fifteen minutes."

"Thank you, Hilda."

She, Fran, Carol and I carried our boxes into the Fremonts' dining room. The long cherry table was bare with the exception of a large fresh centerpiece with mums, daisies and lilies.

Before Hilda left, she turned to Carol. "Did Ms. Martin introduce you as 'Duncan'?"

"Yes, ma'am. I'm Carol Duncan, and this is my daughter Fran."

"Were you related to the young man who died last week?"

"Yes," Carol said. "I'm his aunt."

Hilda nodded. "I'm awfully sorry for your family's loss. He was a good boy, your Fred."

"You knew Fred?" Fran asked.

"Yes, dear. I once showed him a photograph of my poodle Maggie, and he sketched her for me while we waited for our appointments."

"Appointments?" Carol asked.

"Yes. I suppose it won't hurt to spill the beans now. He and I were in a drug research trial together in Abingdon a couple months ago. We were testing a new drug for migraines . . . or, at least, I was. I only discovered I'd had the real thing at the end of the trial."

"Did the medication help you?" I asked.

"Not so much that I could notice," Hilda said. She turned back to Carol. "I framed that sketch. He was a talented young man." She blinked rapidly. "Excuse me, won't you? I'll be in the kitchen should you need anything."

"Thank you, Hilda."

I glanced at Fran and Carol. They appeared to be as perplexed as I was, but we had to put this information on the backburner until after our meeting with Belinda.

"Fran," I said, "would you please plate the cavy cookies and garnish the plate with the marzipan fruit? Carol, let's you and I arrange these cookies in a pretty pattern on this tray."

After preparing the cookies for display, I prepared a crystal pedestal with five white petit-fours bearing golden Fs. We also plated a sampling of candies, fresh fruit, fruit dips and tarts.

We'd barely finished arranging everything when Belinda swept into the dining room with Guinevere in her arms.

"Daphne, darling, this all looks delightful."

"Thank you," I said. "Mrs. Fremont, I'd like to introduce you to Carol and Fran Duncan. They'll be helping me cater your party. I hope you don't mind my bringing them along."

"Certainly not." She nodded at Carol and Fran. "Nice to meet you both. Plus, it's good for you to know up front what will be expected." She turned back to me. "I've been telling

Guinevere about her special cookies, and she's eager to try them."

I took a dessert plate and put two of the cavy cookies on it.

"They're precious," Belinda said. "How did you ever make them so tiny?"

Knowing she didn't really care, I merely smiled and sat the plate onto the table. I pulled out a chair for her, and she sat down.

By this time, Hilda had slipped unobtrusively back into the dining room. She placed a white linen napkin on the table to Belinda's right.

Belinda picked up one of the cookies. Guinevere was leaning toward it before Belinda could get it close enough to her mouth.

"My, you little pig." Belinda looked at me and winked.

We all chuckled like she'd said something ever so clever.

Belinda held the cookie closer to Guinevere, and the "little pig" devoured it and sniffed around for more.

"I believe you have a hit on your hands, Daphne."

"Thank you," I said. "I have an entire plate full here, so you can ensure Lancelot and the rest of Guinevere's friends enjoy them as well."

"Wonderful. Hilda, please take Guinevere up to her room," Belinda said. "Leave the cookies here for now. I'll distribute them at snack time."

"Yes, ma'am." Hilda took the guinea pig.

Guinevere let out a squeak of protest as she was carried from the room. The poor thing wanted another cookie. I couldn't blame her really. I'd tried one last night after Fran and Carol had left. After all, one doesn't serve something to Belinda Fremont—or her cavies—one hasn't sampled first. They weren't bad. And if you were a guinea pig who'd never had a cookie before—who was ignorant of the delights of chocolate chunk, peanut butter and white chocolate macadamia nut—you'd be wanting another one, too.

Belinda spent the next thirty minutes tasting the goodies

and giving me "yays" and "nays." Mostly, there were "yays," thank goodness. And I explained how the various tables would be set up.

"Will the cavies be staying up to usher in the New Year?" I asked.

"No," Belinda said, "I'm afraid it would be a strain on them to deviate that much from their routine."

"What if you have a mini countdown for them near their bedtime?" I asked. "We could even let them drink water out of miniature wine glasses to ring in the New Year. Then we can move them upstairs and get them settled down while the people guests enjoy the remainder of the party."

Belinda clasped her hands together. "Excellent." She smiled. "Daphne, I like the way you think."

*

"Was the Fremont house everything you thought it would be?" I asked Carol as I was driving her and Fran back to their house.

"Everything and more," Carol said. "What a showplace."

"I'll say," Fran said. "Did you see all those guinea pigs' rooms? They were fancier than mine." She drew in a breath. "I mean . . . ."

"It's okay, honey," Carol said. "I know exactly what you mean."

"You know the story in the Bible of the prodigal son?" I asked. "How he squandered his fortune and wound up living with the pigs? That story might've turned out completely different if that boy had gone to live with Belinda's 'pigs.'"

We all laughed.

"Yeah," Carol said. "He might've been more like Joseph during the famine."

"When do you need us to work again?" Fran asked as we neared their house.

"I'm not sure. After I get home and sort through my notes, I'll give you a call so we can work something out," I said.

"Okay." Fran hopped out of the backseat, waved goodbye,

took out her phone and began texting as she strode up the sidewalk.

I shook my head. "No way was I that coordinated at her age."

Carol scoffed. "I'm not that coordinated now."

I smiled. "I'll discuss a tentative schedule with Fran; and if you need to change anything, simply give me a call."

"Thank you. And thanks for taking us with you." She grinned shyly. "I felt like I was visiting Brea Ridge's answer to Biltmore."

"In a way, I guess we were. Belinda modeled her house after Crane Cottage in Jekyll Island, Georgia, and some of the architecture of Crane Cottage was modeled after Biltmore. Apparently, the Cranes and the Vanderbilts were friends."

"Well, how about that. Wait until I tell Pete."

We said our goodbyes, and I drove on home. My mind wandered to Steve Franklin and his brother, and I wondered if China might know anything about their feud. As soon as I got inside, I called her to ask.

"Yeah," she said, "I heard all the gossip about Steve and Robby Franklin . . . oh, I reckon it was ten or fifteen years ago now. What's got you wanting to know about that?"

"Apparently, the reason Fred Duncan was in that car accident last year was because Steve Franklin sent Fred to take his mom flowers for her birthday. Mr. Franklin wouldn't go because his brother was there."

"Yeah, well, that makes sense, I reckon. When I heard over the police scanner that Fred had wrecked on Fox Hollow Road, I was confounded as to why he'd be plumb out there."

"So, what's the deal between Mr. Franklin and his brother?" I asked.

"Well, you see, Steve was sweet on this girl named Erica. They'd dated for several months, and from what I heard told, Steve was fixing to ask her to marry him come Christmas. Then came Thanksgiving break, and Robby came home from college."

"Uh-oh."

"Uh-oh is right. Erica spent Thanksgiving Day with the Franklins, and that night she broke up with Steve. She'd done set her cap for Robby."

"What a hag!" *And I don't mean Hot Available Guy.*

"Well, I agree, dumplin', but Robby Franklin was the kind of man that'd give a woman pause."

"Did Robby get together with Erica?" I asked.

"Yeah, but only for the rest of that weekend. Then he dumped her and told her to go on back to Steve if he was stupid enough to have her back."

"Was he? Was he stupid enough?"

"No. He had the good sense to send her packing. Never got over it, though. Never forgave his brother, and never found a girl to replace Erica."

"So Mr. Franklin never married?"

"Nope. Not unless you count the Save-A-Buck—he seems pretty devoted to that."

"What about Robby?"

"Oh, yeah, he married a darling girl he met after college. I believe they have a couple young 'uns."

"Hmm. He moved on, and Steve didn't," I said.

"Well, that's the thing about forgiveness, dumplin'. You don't forgive somebody that wronged you for their benefit, you do it for yours. All that anger and bitterness has eaten away at Steve Franklin for all these years, but it ain't hurt his brother one iota."

"How about Erica? What ever became of her?"

"She moved away from Brea Ridge is all I know."

"Thanks for filling me in," I said.

"Anytime. Got what happened to Fred figured out yet?"

"I'm afraid not, China."

"Oh, well, you'll get it."

I didn't argue with her. Instead, I told her goodbye and began looking over the notes I'd taken at Belinda's house.

The cavy cookies were a definite yes. I'd need three dozen of those. I'd need two dozen petit-fours. The pinwheels were a no. A cupcake tower using red velvet cupcakes with white icing and raspberry toppers were a yes—I'd need forty of those. And I'd need forty lemon tarts.

I called Fran and told her we could do all the preparations for Belinda's party the five days after Christmas, but three of those days would be fairly labor intensive. "Are you still up for it?"

"You bet," Fran said.

"Do you mean it?" I asked. "I'm not trying to dissuade you, but if you and your mom change your minds and bail on me at the last minute, I'll really be in a pickle."

"We won't bail," Fran said. "Now, while Mom isn't here, we can discuss the investigation."

"Sorry, kiddo, I don't have anything to discuss unless you want to talk about what Hilda, the Fremonts' housekeeper said about meeting Fred at a medical research facility."

"Well, I do think that's odd, but I found out something even stranger than that."

"Okay, shoot."

"None of the food at the Brea Ridge Pharmaceutical Christmas party was contaminated with campylobacter."

"None of it?" *Thank you, God.*

"None of it."

"Are you sure?"

"It was in the toxicology report."

"Wait, wait, wait. Everybody who got sick at the party did test positive for having this particular strain of bacterium in their system, right?"

"Right."

"Then, if it didn't come from the food, where did it come from?" I asked.

"That appears to be the million dollar question."

## Chapter Eleven

"How can that be?" Ben asked when I called him to pass along Fran's information.

"Fran said the police had been back in touch with Connie and told her none of the food tested positive for the campylobacter bacteria."

"Then how did those people get sick?" Ben asked. "Was someone going around passing out free bacteria samples?"

"Now that you mention it, Fran did point out that none of the doctors got sick."

"Daphne, those doctors are not stupid enough to infect a group of partygoers—most of whom are their employees— with a bacterium simply to test a new product. First of all, that would be business suicide. Second, there was no need. The drug had been widely tested, approved and was set to hit the market in January."

"Two excellent points."

"As things stand, the drug release is on hold until Fred's death has been fully investigated and the drug found to have played no part. Instead of looking at the doctors, I think we need to learn who'd want to sabotage them."

"Like a disgruntled employee," I said.

"Or a disgruntled girlfriend."

"I don't know Cara all that well, but that doesn't seem to be her style," I said. "She appears to me more the type who'd merely dump the guy and move on to someone richer and better looking, not ruin the guy's career."

"You didn't think she'd try to get photos of Fred's mom either."

"You've got me there. I'll talk with her and try to get a feel for where she and Doctor Holloway stand."

"Thanks. I'll talk with some of Brea Ridge Pharmaceuticals' employees to see if anyone had a grudge against the company."

After talking with Ben, I called Cara's cell phone. She told me she was back in Richmond until Friday and that she'd give me a call when she got back in town. I said that sounded great. After all, how do you casually ask someone about her current relationship when she's obviously trying to rush you off the phone?

I had plenty of leftover pinwheel cookie dough in the refrigerator; so I baked the cookies, boxed them up and took them—all but one box—to the Save-A-Buck. I took the other box over to Lucas and Leslie, my twin nephew and niece.

Violet hadn't got home from work yet, but my brother-in-law Jason was there. He has a thick head of red hair and a boyish sprinkling of freckles across his face. Lucas and Leslie had taken their blonde hair and blue eyes from Violet.

The instant I walked through the door, Leslie and Lucas swarmed in. Lucas took the cookies while Leslie gave me a crushing hug and asked when we were going Christmas shopping.

"Since I hate going on the weekends this time of year, how about we go Monday morning if it's okay with your mom and dad?" I asked.

"Yay! Lucas," Leslie called, following him to the kitchen. "Aunt Daphne is taking us shopping on Monday."

I could hear their excited chatter as I joined Jason in the living room. "Is that okay with you?"

He grinned. "Of course, it is. Get me something nice."

"Sure. A nice lump of coal."

I caught the pillow he lobbed at me.

He glanced toward the kitchen. "Vi told me about your test-drive. Thanks for that."

"No problem. Actually, it's a lot of fun. You'll love it."

"That's what Vi says." He chuckled. "What I wouldn't have given to have seen you guys over there channeling the Wilson sisters."

"More like the odd couple. Hey, can I ask you something without your mentioning it to my sister?"

A pained expression crossed his face. "Please don't ask me

what to get her for Christmas. I'm still trying to figure that out myself."

"No, it's not that. Do you remember when Fred Duncan had his car wreck last year?"

Jason looked wary, but he nodded.

"Did you ever hear anything about the other driver, the car . . . ?"

"Only the same speculations everyone else heard. I thought you weren't investigating Fred's death."

"I'm not," I said.

He raised his brows.

"Really. I'm not. It's just that his cousin Fran—who's helping me cater Belinda Fremont's New Year's Eve party—was telling me about the accident, and the entire thing sounded really odd."

"It's not that unusual for hit-and-run drivers to get away," he said.

"I know, but what about this Good Samaritan Donald Harper?" I asked. "How is it he was close enough to hear the accident happen but hadn't been close enough to get a tag number or a more accurate description of the car?"

"Daphne, all that stuff is muddy water under a rickety bridge. Let it go. I'm sure Don Harper wishes he could."

"You know Don Harper?"

"Not personally," Jason said, "but after Fred's accident, Brea Ridge divided into two camps—those who saw Don as a hero and those who saw him as a villain."

"A villain? Why?"

"Some people—including Fred's mother—believed that if Don hadn't moved Fred from the car rather than waiting for the ambulance, Fred wouldn't have suffered the brain injury. Others said Don did the right thing and maybe even saved Fred's life."

"What do you think?" I asked.

"I don't know. There was never any evidence that Don's actions contributed to Fred's injuries, and I feel certain his heart was in the right place. Still, it must've been hard for them to work together after that."

"Them who?"

"Don and Fred's mom. They both work at Brea Ridge Pharmaceuticals . . . or, at least, they used to."

Lucas and Leslie barreled into the living room.

"Thanks for the cookies," Lucas said. "They were awesome."

"Were?" Jason asked.

"Yeah," Leslie said. "We saved you one, but you'd better hurry and get it before Mom gets here."

"And throw away the box," Lucas said.

"Or put it back in Aunt Daphne's car," Leslie said. "Either way, we figure you don't want Mom to know you let us eat a box of cookies before dinner."

"Let you?" Jason asked.

"I'm all for putting the box in Aunt Daphne's car," Lucas said. "That way, she can put something else in it and bring it next time she comes. Come on, Dad. Get your cookie, so I can put the box in the car."

As Lucas hustled Jason off to the kitchen, Leslie flopped onto the couch and gave me a Cheshire cat smile.

"So which mall are we going to?" she asked.

"Which mall do you want to go to?" I had little enough sense to ask.

"The ginormous mall in Sevierville. Where else?"

*

Instead of going home, I headed to the local mall. While I could shop for everyone else with Leslie and Lucas in tow, I certainly couldn't shop for them. With everything else going on, I thought tonight was as good a night as any to shop for my favorite gift recipients.

I parked under a street lamp and walked briskly to the nearest entrance. Fran was right—I do take this crime stuff seriously. Once you've been a victim of domestic abuse, your radar and defenses are always on high-alert.

I entered the mall and went straight to the video game store. I bought Lucas and Leslie each a video game and was on route to the hobby shop when I met John Holloway.

I smiled. "It seems we're both on a mission, Dr. Holloway."

"Indeed." He nodded toward the bag I was carrying and then indicated his empty hands. "But it appears you're having more success than I am."

"Maybe my mission is easier."

"Cara isn't the easiest person to buy for," he said. "Have you eaten dinner yet?"

"No, I haven't."

"Would you care to join me for a sandwich in the food court? Maybe you and I can brainstorm this gift dilemma."

"I'd enjoy that."

We rode down the escalator to the food court. The festive decorations and Christmas carols were uplifting. And, I had to admit, I was glad for the serendipity that had given me and John Holloway the opportunity to chat one-on-one.

After conferring with me, Dr. Holloway got us both a chicken sandwich and a soft drink. We sat at one of the black wrought iron bistro tables and opened our sandwiches.

"It must be difficult for you and Cara to be apart so much of the time," I said.

"We've adjusted. After all, we knew when we met that our careers were based in separate parts of the state."

"How did you meet?"

"I was at a conference in Richmond. Cara was there covering the event for the *West Side Messenger*. After my keynote address, she asked if she could buy me a coffee in the hotel café to further discuss the topic of genome research. I accepted, and a little over a year later, here we are."

"That's terrific."

"What about you and Ben?"

"We've known each other since we were children," I said. "We lost touch when we went off to college, but we reconnected when I moved back to Brea Ridge."

He smiled. "That's a wonderful story. The two of you have quite a bit of history, and yet you've both grown so much in the intervening years, there's so much new you both bring to a relationship."

"Yes, I guess that's true." I took a drink of my soda. "Dr. Holloway, can I ask you something about the Christmas party?" I help up a hand. "I'm not trying to step on toes or scoop stories or any of that sort of thing, but Fran—a relative of Fred Duncan—told me none of the food served at the party tested positive for the campylobacter bacterium. Do you think someone was trying to harm the people at the party or, perhaps, the pharmaceutical company itself?"

"We have our security people looking into that, Daphne. It's confounding to me. Sure, we have samples of many different bacteria in the lab, but it's securely locked away."

"Still, your employees have access," I said.

"Most of them do. But why would they want it?" He frowned. "Please let's discuss gifts. I really want to put this current mess out of my head for now."

"Of course, you do. I'm sorry I brought it up. Do you have any children in your life—nieces, nephews, young siblings?"

"No, I'm sorry I don't. You?"

"Yes. I have a fabulous niece and nephew. They're the brightest spots in my life and who I'm out shopping for this evening. The three of us are planning a shopping excursion of our own on Monday, so I'm shopping for them now."

"Good idea. Sorry I can't be of any help. Still, I'm fairly certain they'll drop all sorts of hints while the three of you are out shopping."

I laughed. "You've got a point. But, then, they've been dropping hints since July!"

He laughed, too. "If only Cara would drop a hint or two."

"I'm guessing you want to get her both a practical gift and a romantic, impulsive one. Am I right?"

"Absolutely. Suggestions?"

"I know she adores coffee," I said. "Does she have one of those personal coffee making systems? You know, the ones that use pods? I have one, and I love it."

"That's a fantastic idea, and I don't think she has one of those. What else have you got?"

"Well, there's always jewelry."

Here Dr. Holloway looked a bit pensive. "Please don't say anything about this to Cara, but I'm afraid she might be expecting more than I'm willing to offer at this point."

"You think she might be expecting an engagement ring?"

He nodded. "And I don't feel we're ready for that step. To be involved in a long-distance relationship is one thing; a long-distance marriage is another."

\*

When I got home, I wrapped my gifts to Leslie and Lucas and placed them under the Christmas tree. It was nice to have presents beneath the tree at last.

Myra came over. "I know it's getting a little late," she said, "but I thought we could play us a song or two."

I smiled. "Sure, Myra. Come on in."

"Hey, you finally got some packages under that tree. I'm proud of you."

"Thanks."

As I was starting up the game, the phone rang.

"My, my, you work quickly," Cara said when I answered. "This morning I told you I was out of town until Friday, and this evening you have dinner with my boyfriend."

I laughed. "That *was* quite a coincidence, wasn't it?"

"Quite." She wasn't laughing.

"He told me you and he met while he was in Richmond at a genome research convention."

"Yeah. Look, I like you, Daphne, but please don't get in my way."

"In your way? Cara, I wouldn't dream of interfering with your—"

"Yeah, well, I have to run. See you on Friday." With that, she hung up.

I replaced the receiver and turned to Myra. "That was weird."

"What was weird?" she asked. "You know how I love

weird."

"There's a reporter from Richmond who's dating John Holloway of Brea Ridge Pharmaceuticals."

"The blonde who was on TV the other morning talking about Ben being sick?"

"That's the one." *Am I the only person in Brea Ridge who sleeps past five a.m.?* "Anyway, she and I became acquainted a couple months ago. I called her this morning, and she said she would be out of town until Friday. Then it just so happened that Dr. Holloway and I ran into each other in the mall."

"And Blondie's nose is out of joint because of that?"

"Well, we did have a sandwich together at the food court," I said.

"Did you go Dutch, or did he buy?"

"He bought, but it was perfectly innocent."

"Perfectly innocent to you maybe, but I can see why Blondie is concerned. The minute she goes out of town, Dagwood is buying dinner for Rachel Ray."

"It wasn't like that. We met purely by accident and had a meal together so he could have me give him suggestions on what to buy Cara for Christmas."

"Still, he fed you. Blondie might not be the only gal for him."

"Oh, come on, Myra. I feed you all the time, and we're not dating. And I even give you homemade baked goods."

"You've got a point. But if Carl was still alive, I might be a little leery of you."

I put my hands on my hips and glared at her.

"Well, look at you," she continued. "You're beautiful, you're talented and you make some of the best food I've ever eaten. Why, my Carl would've wept at your feet."

I got tickled. "Oh, he would not have. He loved you very much. And as far as Cara is concerned, look at her. She's gorgeous, has an exciting career . . . ."

"True, but that's no sign she isn't insecure." She jerked her head toward the television set. "Let's rock."

And rock we did. Finally, I suggested hot chocolate and

biscotti.

"Sounds like a winner," Myra said. "What's on your mind?"

"What do you mean, what's on my mind?"

"Generally, when you break out the hot beverage and dessert, you're mulling over something. What is it?"

"Am I really that predictable?"

Myra shrugged.

We went into the kitchen. She sat down at the table while I heated milk for the hot chocolate.

"It's the Brea Ridge Pharmaceutical party," I said. "Fran told me today that none of the food served at the party made those people sick."

"Then why did they get sick?"

"That's just it. They had to have come in contact with the bacterium somewhere onsite."

"What I can't figure out is why they'd have the party at the company instead of somewhere nice like Dakota's in the first place," Myra said. "Whoever heard tell of having a Christmas party in a place where they manufacture drugs? That makes about as much sense as having a Valentine's Day dance in a crack house. But, then, I reckon that could happen, too. Crack heads are people just like the rest of us . . . except they're crack heads. I reckon they fall in love and celebrate Valentine's Day, too."

I finished making the hot chocolate and poured us each a mug. I sat the mugs and the biscotti on the table and pulled out a chair.

"I doubt they're all that thoughtful about gift-giving, though," Myra said. "They probably just give each other crack. Or, I guess in some instances, it could be like an O.Henry story. 'But, sugar puss, I sold my crack pipe to buy you some crack.' 'And I sold *my* crack pipe to buy *you* some crack.' Then they'd get teary-eyed and embrace, and the audience would share a collective 'awww.'"

I decided to play along. "What if they realize they have each other, no longer need crack and check into a rehab clinic together?"

"But on the way there, they start having withdrawals so bad they fly into a rage and kill each other?" She nodded. "That'd make a good screenplay. It could serve as a warning to young lovers everywhere."

"Well, then . . . . Let me know if you write that."

"I will. And you know who'd be great in the man's part? Johnny Depp. He can play about any role they give him. And nearly any of those little anorexic starlets could play the girl."

"Okay then. Jason was telling me this afternoon that after Fred Duncan's car accident, half the town believed Don Harper was a hero, and the other half saw him as a villain. What did you think?"

Myra sipped her hot chocolate and seemed to consider how to best frame her response. "I think Don's heart was in the right place. But I believe he should've left the boy where he was. People that don't know what they're doing can do more harm than good in a situation like that."

"But I thought Mr. Harper was a trained paramedic."

"Well, I don't know how much training he'd had, but I do know that when China's daughter-in-law was in a car accident, two EMTs strapped her to a backboard and got her out of the car because they were scared she'd hurt her head or neck." She waved her biscotti. "So I know there's regulations and protocols and stuff like that. And that car wasn't on fire or anything. Don Harper should've waited instead of trying to be Superman."

I slowly nodded. She had a point. She also had a point about why Dr. Broadstreet would have the party catered at the office. Why not his home, a restaurant or a conference center? Maybe I should talk with Dr. Broadstreet and find out.

## Chapter Twelve

On Wednesday morning, I started my day at Brea Ridge Pharmaceuticals. I took a loaf of oatmeal cinnamon bread with a business card affixed to the top of the box.

"Hello," I said to the receptionist. Her back was turned; but when she faced me, I could see she was a former high school classmate. "Helen!"

"Why, Daphne Carter, when did you move back to Brea Ridge?"

"Just a couple months ago." I started to tell her my last name was "Martin" now, but then she'd ask who I'd married, if I had any children and countless other questions I'd prefer not to answer. "Is Dr. Broadstreet available? I don't need but about two minutes of his time."

"Let me check and see if he's busy." She walked away from the desk and stepped down the hall.

Although Dr. Broadstreet had ordered the cake for the Christmas party, I'd never actually met him. He'd ordered the cake over the phone, I'd delivered it the afternoon of the party and I'd received my check in the mail.

"Dr. Broadstreet will see you," Helen said when she returned to the window. She pressed a button and a green light came on over the door to her right. "You may come on in."

I opened the door and went through to Helen's office. The door shut behind me with a clang.

"Oops," I said. "I didn't mean to let the door slam."

"That's okay. All the doors here slam. They're heavy and automatic, and they're loud. These guys are big on security."

"They deal with a lot of sensitive stuff, I guess."

"You're telling me. That's why I keep a big bottle of hand sanitizer on my desk at all times and one in my purse."

"Were you at the Christmas party?" I asked.

"No way, and thank goodness I wasn't."

"Really. I'll talk with you again in a sec. I don't want to

keep Dr. Broadstreet waiting."

"Right. He's straight down this hall, second door on your left."

"Great. Thanks, Helen."

I followed Helen's instructions and knocked on Dr. Broadstreet's door. He called for me to come in.

He was a large man with a florid face, heavy black-rimmed glasses, white hair combed back to reveal a high forehead and a full beard. He was wearing a white lab coat over a yellow T-shirt. His office was half lab, half office—all mess. I wondered how he ever found anything in this room. Test tubes, beakers, microscopes and papers cluttered the counter against the wall to the right. Papers, files, notebooks and more beakers cluttered the desk.

"Yes? What can I do for you? Didn't you get your check?"

"Indeed, I did, Dr. Broadstreet, and I merely wanted to stop by and thank you for your business." I handed him the box containing the oatmeal cinnamon bread.

"What's this?"

"Just a little thank-you gift . . . oatmeal cinnamon bread."

By the time I got those words out of my mouth, Dr. Broadstreet had a bite of oatmeal cinnamon bread in his.

"Delicious," he said with his mouth full and his beard dotted with crumbs.

"Thank you. Please keep me in mind for future baking and catering needs."

"I shall do that, young lady." He pinched off another piece of the bread and popped it in his mouth. "Anything else?"

"No, sir. Um . . . enjoy the bread. My business card is on the top of the box."

He simply waved and kept eating.

Okay, so I didn't have the guts to come right out and ask him why he'd host a Christmas party in a pharmaceutical cafeteria. By the way he'd delved into that bread, I took it he wasn't terribly particular about when and where he ate. Besides, I'd probably make more headway on that topic by talking with Helen.

I saw a sign with an arrow pointing toward "Accounting." Remembering that Connie was the bookkeeper here, I thought I'd drop in very quickly to see how she was doing today. When I opened the door to the accounting department, a man was standing in front of the filing cabinets thumbing through a file. He was tall and slender with gray-streaked brown hair and a thick but neatly-trimmed moustache.

"Can I help you with something?" he asked.

"Please. I was here visiting Dr. Broadstreet, and I wanted to stop by and see Connie Duncan before I left."

"Connie stepped into another office," he said, "but she should be back any minute. You're welcome to wait."

"Thank you. I'm Daphne Martin."

He stretched out his arm and shook my hand. "Pleasure to meet you, Daphne. I'm Don Harper."

"Don Harper. I recognize your name from a newspaper account I read about Fred Duncan's car accident."

"You must have some memory. That accident happened well over a year ago."

"Still, you were quite the hero."

He grunted. "Not everybody shares your opinion, Daphne."

"I'm sorry to hear that. What an ordeal that entire day must've been for you."

"You can say that again. That's one time I wish I'd minded my own business and not got involved in any of it." He returned the file to the cabinet and slammed the drawer shut. "I'd better get back to work." He strode into the office labeled "comptroller" and closed the door.

I decided not to wait for Connie after all. I went back out front and said goodbye to Helen.

"Thanks for all your help," I said. "I really appreciate Brea Ridge Pharmaceuticals' business." I leaned in and lowered my voice conspiratorially. "Although why they decided to have their party here is beyond me."

"I'll tell you why," Helen said. "This place is bleeding money, and they don't have any bandages big enough to make it stop. Two drug companies pulled their funding for research, and there are fewer government grants available right now to help offset costs. Personally, I'm keeping my options open just in case. If you hear of anyone who's hiring . . . ."

"I'll let you know," I said.

"Thanks. Oh, and Merry Christmas, Daphne."

"You, too, Helen."

*

On the way home, I called Fran to see if she could help me get some baking done. She said she could and that she'd meet me at my house.

I got there first and put my hair up, slipped on my apron and washed my hands. I was making peanut butter fudge when Fran got there.

"We're making candy today," I said, "for Save-A-buck and for our families."

"Our families? I get some, too?"

"Of course. But don't worry, you're still getting paid."

"Are you kidding? That's the least of my worries. I'm just thrilled to be able to take something home and show off what I helped make."

"By the end of the day, you'll have lots to take home and show off." I stirred the fudge, which was almost ready to pour into the pan. "Besides this fudge, we'll be making cake balls, chocolate-covered coconut candy, white and milk chocolate dipped strawberries, haystacks, macadamia brittle and maple fudge."

"I'm gaining weight simply thinking about it."

I smiled. I was thinking *as if,* but I didn't say it. "We'll be packaging the candy in small boxes of individual types and larger boxes of assorted candies." I poured the fudge into a large pan and sat it in the refrigerator to set. "Now let's do the cake balls."

"What on earth are cake balls?" Fran asked.

"You know how I sometimes carve cakes into particular shapes?"

Fran nodded.

"Instead of wasting the cake trimmed away, I use it to make cake balls. Here, I'll show you."

I took a freezer bag of cake trimmings from the counter where they'd been thawing. These pieces were chocolate, marble and white. I divided the cake trimmings into various flavors. I had a small bowl of chocolate butter cream and a small bowl of vanilla butter cream. I slipped on plastic gloves and handed the box to Fran so she could do the same.

"Start tearing the white into smaller bits please," I said, starting on the chocolate. "Put the pieces into the vanilla frosting." I put the chocolate cake into the chocolate frosting.

I showed Fran how to mix the cake and frosting together with her hands until she could form one-inch balls from the mixture. It's messy but by no means difficult; and within minutes, we had two dozen chocolate cake balls and two dozen white cake balls. We divided the marble cake, using white frosting for one dozen and chocolate frosting for the other.

"Cool," Fran said. "Now what?"

"Now we put them in the freezer for a few minutes so they'll set up enough to dip in chocolate. We could use white, dark or milk chocolate; but I thought we'd use milk chocolate and then roll the balls in white sprinkles."

"Are they as good as they sound?" Fran asked.

"Better." I took off my gloves and tossed them into the garbage can. I then slid the trays into the freezer and sat on a stool at the island.

Fran threw her gloves away and took a seat on the other stool. "Remember the football player I was telling you about the other day? He came to Fred's funeral."

"That was nice."

She smiled slightly. "Yeah, it was. I might invite him over to have some of these cake balls." She looked down at her hands. "He did say he was there if I needed to talk."

"That was *very* nice."

"Yeah. I didn't want to mention that in front of Mom. You don't think that's taking advantage of Fred's death, do you?"

"No. I think he reached out to you during a sad time and that if you want to call him up and thank him for that, it would be perfectly all right. And then, if he asks you out, or if you want to invite him over for dinner with you and your parents or something, that would be all right, too."

"Thanks, Daphne."

"Now let me ask you something. Did your aunt think it was strange that Brea Ridge Pharmaceuticals had their Christmas party at the office, or was it customary to have it there?"

"They usually have their parties at the Brea Ridge Inn's banquet hall or at a restaurant in Bristol. But they said things were a little tighter this year. They had you make the cake, of course, but Dr. Broadstreet's wife made everything else."

"She must've been a wreck when everyone got sick."

"She got sick, too. But I guess it did worry her to think it could've been her food that made everyone sick . . . which, of course, is what everybody thought until the police told us it wasn't."

"That makes me wonder . . . ."

"What?" Fran asked. "What are you wondering?"

"I'm wondering if Dr. Broadstreet or one of the other doctors would contaminate something else with the bacterium so they could pull out their terrific new drug, become heroes, get a lot of good publicity and have the money start rolling back into the company."

"I don't know about Dr. Broadstreet. I mean, with his wife making the food, wouldn't everybody automatically suspect her first?"

"Yeah. But what do we know about the other doctors? What do we know about Dr. Broadstreet, for that matter? Maybe the guy hates his wife, and he saw this as an opportunity to take care of his financial problems and his marital problems at the same time."

"True," Fran said, "but that doesn't seem likely since the bacterium wasn't found in the food."

I nodded. Connie would have a lot better insight into the

doctors and which of them—if any—might be driven to pull a stunt like this. I'd promised Violet I wouldn't investigate the case anymore, though. And Fran's mother didn't want *her* investigating the case. I tapped my fingernails on the island.

"What are you thinking?"

"I'm thinking Connie could help us out on this one. This thought might have even crossed her mind already." I shrugged.

"I'll stop by her house and talk with her on the way home."

"What will your mom say?"

"She'll think I was terribly sweet to stop by with some candy for Aunt Connie." She batted her eyes and smiled.

I laughed. Okay, I know I shouldn't be encouraging her. But encouraging and refraining from discouraging are actually two different things. Aren't they?

*

I packed up the boxes of candy I was taking to Save-A-Buck and placed them in the backseat of the car. I went back to get the invoice I'd left on the counter. When I stepped back onto the porch, Sparrow rubbed against my legs. I bent and stroked her head, and she purred.

*I'll get you moved in soon*, I thought, my mind conjuring up an image of the cat coming to the door with her worldly possessions wrapped in a bandana and tied to a stick.

When I arrived at the store, I retrieved a cart and stacked the boxes of candy in it. I'd printed labels with the candies' names and ingredients and placed the labels on the clear boxes. I have a computer program that will also provide nutritional information, but I didn't include that. Who wants to think about calories at Christmas? I know I don't.

Mr. Franklin met me at the door. "Goodness! It appears Save-A-Buck customers have hit the jackpot today."

"I hope they'll agree."

"After you get those arranged on the display table, come on back to my office. I have a check for the birthday cakes and some other items that have sold this week."

"Great. I'll be there in a few minutes."

Very little of what I'd brought in last week and earlier this week remained on the table that served as Save-A-Buck's bakery. I rearranged the items that did remain to accommodate the boxes of candy.

Once I had the display looking suitable, I went to Mr. Franklin's office to get my check. I tapped on the office door, and he called for me to come in. I'd been rehearsing a faux conversation with Mr. Franklin while I'd worked on the bakery display, but I was a bit nervous about starting the conversation for real.

I walked in and sat on a vinyl chair near the door. "Don't mind me," I said. "I just popped in to get the check, but you go ahead and finish up what you're doing." I glimpsed a game of solitaire open on his computer screen. "I don't want to interrupt."

"I'm . . . I'm not that busy at the moment. Let me take care of this one thing." He minimized the window. "There."

I gave a loud sigh. "Mr. Franklin, do you have any brothers or sisters?"

"Why do you ask?"

"Just curious." I sighed again. "I love my sister dearly, but she can be a total pain. I've always felt like Violet was the golden child in my mother's eyes . . . the one who did everything right. And then Mom has me—the disappointment. In some ways, it makes me dread holidays."

"I know what you mean. I have a brother—Robby— who's older, more sophisticated, more successful . . . more everything."

"Does he live here in Brea Ridge?"

Mr. Franklin shook his head. "He lives in Boone. He went to Appalachian State and then got a job there in town when he graduated."

"What does he do?"

"Retail management."

"Same as you. Cool. At least, you have some common ground, right?"

He looked at me for a second and then smirked. "Yeah."

The polite thing would've been to let it go at that point. But I wasn't being polite. I was digging for information. So I said, "That didn't sound very convincing. Do the two of you have different management styles?"

"Yeah. I use the small management style, while he employs the large regional chain style of management."

"Aren't you being a little hard on yourself? You operate the only independently-owned—heck the *only*—grocery store in Brea Ridge, and that's an impressive accomplishment."

"You can say that because you've never met Robby—or Robert, as he calls himself now."

"I don't believe that. No matter what your brother has done, he can't belittle your accomplishments . . . and you shouldn't either. You need to remind yourself of all Robby's mistakes and failures," I said. "Hasn't he ever screwed up?"

As Mr. Franklin slowly nodded, his eyes filled with tears. Blinking furiously, he spun back around to the computer. He plucked an envelope from the corner of the desk and, without looking away from the computer, handed it to me. "Thank you, Ms. Martin."

"Thank you, Mr. Franklin."

## Chapter Thirteen

I was tired when I got home. I didn't feel like baking any more this evening. Instead, I took a bath, slipped into some comfy flannel pjs and curled up on the sofa with the photo album I'd filled with photographs I'd taken at the 2009 Oklahoma Sugar Art Show. Tucked between a couple back pages of the photo album was the manila envelope containing the articles Cara had sent me reporting on the event.

She was a good reporter. She really brought situations and the people involved to life. In one portion of the article, she told about a contestant's mad rush to get his cake to the event in time to qualify for entry.

*He was pushing it, and his reckless driving attested to that. He even cut this reporter off in traffic, and I called the phone number listed on the van to report him to his superior. Unfortunately, he was the superior. However, the girl who answered the phone said she was sorry and she was sure "Dad" hadn't cut me off like that on purpose.*

*Poor "Dad." Luck wasn't with him today. Whatever had conspired to keep him from the competition further bedeviled him after he arrived at the show. Either damaged en route, or via "spectator damage" as alleged, some breakage occurred prior to the judging, causing "Dad" to suffer a disheartening loss.*

Reading that, my mind flashed back to Cara warning me not to get in her way. Had she been angry enough with the guy in the van that she sabotaged his cake? Or was I merely jumping to conclusions?

Knowing there was one person who knew everything that happened at the Oklahoma Sugar Art Show and who didn't draw conclusions lightly, I went to my office and got out Kerry Vincent's business card. Before I lost my nerve, I placed the call. Expecting to reach an answering machine, I was surprised when Mrs. Vincent answered the phone.

"Mrs. Vincent, this is Daphne Martin calling. We met at the Oklahoma Sugar Art Show a couple months ago."

"Ah, yes, the young woman from Virginia who was afraid to enter the competition."

"Um . . . yes . . . that's me. The reason I'm calling is to ask if you recall a reporter who covered the Sugar Art Show. Her name was Cara Logan."

"Of course, I remember that nasty piece of work from Richmond. Why do you ask?"

"A few minutes ago, I was rereading her article detailing the events of the show. She told about a man who'd cut her off in traffic and whose cake later suffered breakage. I thought that was quite a coincidence."

"Coincidence, my eye," Mrs. Vincent said. "She's the one who ruined that cake. I'm sure of it. She was furious when she arrived at the expo building and demanded to see me. One of the volunteers tracked me down—no easy feat, I assure you, as I'm being pulled in a hundred different directions during that time—and I went with her to where Ms. Logan waited, tapping her food impatiently."

"Based on my encounters with Cara Logan, that sounds about right."

"She insisted I throw David Barrows from the competition because of a silly traffic infraction that hadn't even resulted in an accident. Naturally, I refused. When David's cake was damaged later that day, I immediately knew who'd done it although I couldn't prove it. The cakes are judged anonymously. No one knows whose is whose until the competition. Of course, if she was watching him unload his van, she'd have known which cake was his. Unfortunately, nobody had seen the crafty shrew actually sabotaging the cake."

"But you're certain she's the one who did it?"

"I'm positive. In fact, she came just short of admitting it. Since I had no actual proof, I didn't have security escort her off the premises, but I did have them keep a close watch on her for the remainder of the show."

"Thank you, Mrs. Vincent. I appreciate your taking the time to talk with me."

"Anytime, Daphne. I hope to see you at next year's show. And if you run across Cara Logan, give her a wide berth. She's nothing but trouble."

"Thank you. I will."

After speaking with Mrs. Vincent, I did an Internet search for Cara Logan. A cake decorators' discussion forum had a thread wherein members shared Mrs. Vincent's conviction that Cara had purposefully ruined David Barrows' cake.

A blogger on an entirely different subject had referred to Cara as "Hurricane Cara," saying, "She blew into town to cover a gubernatorial scandal and left a path of destruction a mile wide behind her when she left." Another site had put Cara on a watch list of reporters who could not be trusted.

I found links to some of Cara's own articles containing inflammatory comments and suggestions like those about the van driver and his cake being damaged. Even if Cara hadn't broken that piece of lattice off David Barrows' cake herself, how many vindicating coincidences did one person get? Did Cara know John Holloway was not planning to propose to her and had released the bacterium as some sort of preemptive strike? Or was I simply jumping to conclusions because I'd been insulted by Cara's warning not to get in her way?

I logged off the computer and returned to the living room. I sat on the couch, put my feet up and covered myself with an afghan. Taking the position Cara did want to punish Dr. Holloway for not proposing: one, how could she be sure he wouldn't propose; two, how could she get through the company's security measures; and, three, how would she know the proper way to distribute the bacterium without infecting herself?

No, it had to have been someone on the inside. If not one of the doctors, then someone who knew how to safely handle toxic substances . . . and how to quickly and effectively infect a room full of select people.

\*

Thursday morning after I'd showered and dressed, I sat down in the club chair in the living room to enjoy my second cup of coffee. There were several things I wanted and needed to get done today. As I began cataloguing them in my mind, the doorbell rang. I peeped out the window and saw Fran's car in the driveway.

I went into the kitchen and opened the door. "Good morning. You're out awfully early."

"I know." Fran held a large gift bag out to me. "I wanted to see if you needed any baking help today, and I wanted to bring you this. It's from Aunt Connie."

"What is it?" I asked, taking the bag and placing it on the island so I could hang up Fran's coat.

"Open it and see."

"All right." I carefully opened the bag. It contained the sketch Fred had made of me, and it had been beautifully matted and framed. I clasped it to my chest. "I love it." I looked at it again before clutching it to myself once more. "I really love it. This means so much to me."

"I know." Fran nodded. "She gave me mine, too. She said it was to thank us . . . you know, for our work on Fred's behalf."

"That was completely unnecessary," I said, "but I'm happy to have this."

I took the sketch into the living room and hung it on the wall to the left of the armoire. I turned to Fran. "I'll call Connie later today and thank her." I nodded toward the sofa. "Let's chat."

After we were both seated—Fran on the sofa and me on the club chair—I began our conversation.

"Did you really come over to bake today or did you come to relay the information you gleaned from your Aunt Connie yesterday evening?"

Fran gave me a sheepish grin. "Both."

"All right. So tell me what you've got."

"Well, first of all, I want you to know she loved the cake balls. My whole family did. They loved all the treats I brought home last night. In fact, Mom had to put some in the freezer because she was afraid Dad would eat them all, and we wouldn't have any for Christmas."

"That's great."

"Plus, they were really proud of me for helping to make them, and I had to promise my mom that I'd show her how to make cake balls. And, do you know what else?"

She didn't breathe long enough for me to ask what else.

"The football player I was telling you about—the one who's a total HAG—I took your advice and called to thank him for coming to Fred's funeral, and he's stopping by tomorrow afternoon. How cool is that?"

This time she did pause long enough for me to interject. "That's really cool. Did your Aunt Connie happen to mention whether or not she believes Dr. Broadstreet and his wife are on good terms?"

"Aunt Connie said the Broadstreets are really odd birds and, like, complete opposites as a couple. He's big and sloppy and kind of . . . what was the word she used? Repugnant, I think is what she said. Mrs. Broadstreet, on the other hand, is Kate Moss thin, a vegan and as twitchy as a nervous rabbit." She giggled. "I'm not kidding—that's exactly how Aunt Connie described this lady. When I asked what she meant about the twitchy thing, she said, 'Her eyes are always darting everywhere like she's afraid someone or something is about to jump out at her.' Aunt Connie said she believes if anyone were to look at the poor woman and say 'boo', she'd either pee her pants or faint dead away." Fran giggled again. "I know that's kinda sad, but Aunt Connie's description was funny, too."

"Wonder what Mrs. Broadstreet is so nervous about?" I asked.

Fran shrugged. "Who knows?"

"Maybe we can visit her soon and get a better read on her. Did your Aunt Connie say anything about any of the other doctors or anyone else she works with?"

"Not a lot. She mentioned this—Fred's death, I'm sure is what she meant but she just wasn't able to say that exactly—is a major roadblock to the drug hitting the market and Brea Ridge Pharmaceuticals getting the financial boost it so desperately needed. She said most of the people she works with are walking on egg shells around her because they seem to be afraid she'll sue the company and they'll either be called to testify or that the suit will bankrupt the company, and they'll all be without jobs."

"Poor Connie." I thought a second. "But you said *most* of the people are walking on egg shells. Who isn't?"

"Don Harper. She said he's treating her the same as always and is even acting like nothing ever happened."

"Did your Aunt Connie say it was hard to work with Don given the way she felt about his behavior after Fred's wreck?" I asked.

"She told me the first couple months after the accident, she and Don shared a hostility that was always just below the surface. Of course, that made it almost impossible for them to work together, and they're in the same department. Their supervisor noticed it and said if they couldn't learn to work together again, they'd both be fired. Aunt Connie said that ever since then, she and Mr. Harper have worked together with a begrudging tolerance."

"It's odd the supervisor was threatening to fire them both," I said. "Wouldn't the supervisor normally blame the subordinate for making all the trouble and simply fire the one person?"

Fran shook her head. "Some employers might try to do that—after all, we learned in government class that Virginia is an at-will employer state and that anyone can be let go at any time—but Brea Ridge Pharmaceuticals detests law suits and avoids them at all costs . . . which is why they didn't fire Aunt Connie, who is below Don Harper on the basis of seniority."

"Do you think that's the outcome—firing Connie—Don Harper was hoping for?"

"Sure, he was. I mean, playing devil's advocate here, wouldn't you? The guy did what he thought was a good deed only to have a person he works closely with on a daily basis believe he caused her son's brain injury."

"And then the company didn't have his back either," I

said, "which makes Mr. Harper angry with both Connie and Brea Ridge Pharmaceuticals."

*

Later that afternoon, Ben stopped by with a pizza and a movie.

"I hope you don't have other plans," he said.

"Actually, I have a date," I said with a grin. "I didn't know it until I opened the door, but hey, I'll take what I can get."

Ben smiled. "I'm sorry to drop in on you like this. I know it was presumptuous of me, but I've missed you." He shrugged. "So I took a chance that you'd be home and wouldn't be busy."

"Well, you're in luck," I said, grabbing a couple plates, sodas and forks. I turned back to Ben. "I've missed you, too." I cocked my head to try to read the title of the movie on the DVD spine. "What're we watching?"

"It's an adventure movie. I know how you like Nicolas Cage."

"Great. Would you like to eat in here in the kitchen, and then I'll make us some popcorn to have with the movie? That way, we'll have more of an opportunity to talk."

"All right. Sounds like a winner to me."

We sat down at the kitchen table with the pizza box between us.

"Thanks for cooking," I said.

"Anytime." He opened the box and put a slice of the meat pizza on each of our plates.

"You look good," I said. "You must be feeling better."

"Good as new. What've you been up to these past couple days?"

I'm not sure he didn't regret opening that flood gate. I told him about my trip to Brea Ridge Pharmaceuticals, what Fran had learned from Connie and about running into Dr. Holloway at the mall.

"I'd no more than got home when Cara called and warmed me not to get in her way," I said. "Can you believe that? I mean, Dr. Holloway was asking me to help him come up with a Christmas gift *for her*, for goodness' sake." I started to continue but realized I must be sounding like Fran. I'd spent quite a bit of time with her this week, and her rapid-fire machine gun style of storytelling was starting to rub off on me.

"It sounds like you've had quite a week. Unfortunately, I went back to work and had a ton of paperwork on my desk. Besides that, I've had a number of articles to edit—all on a tight deadline, naturally—so I haven't had much time to investigate Fred's death."

"I told you Myra and I went to the medical research clinic in Haysi, didn't I?"

Ben nodded, cutting into his second slice of pizza with his fork. "But I thought they wouldn't tell you anything."

"They wouldn't, but I'm more positive than ever that Fred was a test subject there."

"Why's that?"

I told Ben about Hilda, the Fremonts' housekeeper, saying she'd met Fred at the medical research clinic in Abingdon. "They were both in a trial there for a medicine used to treat migraines. She told me, Carol and Fran about meeting Fred when they were both there for their appointments."

"Fred had migraines?" Ben asked. "Were they because of his accident?"

"I don't know. I didn't discuss it with Connie; and if Fran or Carol did, they didn't mention it to me. But later that night, I did an Internet search for medical drug research trials and learned there are people who do that on a regular basis." I took a bite of my pizza. I was still on my first slice, and it was starting to get cold.

"What do you mean a regular basis?"

"There are people who submit themselves for drug research on a regular basis. Some even make part-time or full-time jobs out of it."

"But why?" Ben asked.

"Some of the research trials pay really well."

"Still, isn't that dangerous?"

"It can be. The drug testers—often referred to as guinea

pigs—move around so they're not always at the same research center. I think there are some strict rules about how long they're supposed to wait before engaging in new trials and things like that, but the professionals know how to get around the rules."

Ben frowned. "Do you think Hilda is one of these professional drug testers?"

"No, no, no . . . not Hilda. She was merely seeking treatment for her migraines. From the information I read, there are many Hildas in the system—people who are seeking help for their specific problems. On the other hand, some academic-based research centers even test on medical students; and some of the trials are bizarre. For example, one study I read about tested how cocaine was metabolized by the human body. Tell me that isn't dangerous."

"You have to be kidding," Ben said.

"I'm afraid I'm not."

"And people actually sign up for things like this to make a profit?"

I nodded. "Yeah, one guy said he signed up for the cocaine test in college where he was a medical student and thought, 'Hey, I'm getting paid to take illegal drugs.'"

"Unbelievable."

"Fran said Fred wanted to buy Connie something really nice for Christmas. I think he somehow got into this as a way to make money on the side," I said. "And I think it might be— at least, in part—why he's dead."

## Chapter Fourteen

After Ben had gone home to Sally—his golden retriever—I couldn't get Fred, Cara and the entire Brea Ridge Pharmaceutical situation out of my mind. I began to wonder if Cara was reporting on the events yet. If her newspaper was footing her travel bills, then she should be reporting on them. After all, she'd been down here most of last week and had told me she'd be back tomorrow. Even if she couldn't tie the entire case up into a tidy little bow, she had to be giving the publisher and editor something. Why else would they let her come back and expend their resources for a story going nowhere?

I made myself a mug of sugar-free cocoa with mini marshmallows and went into my office. As I waited for the computer to boot up, I thought about my promise to Violet and my upcoming shopping trip with Leslie and Lucas.

*I do not need to be involved in this investigation.*

I logged onto the Internet and typed *West Side Messenger + Richmond, VA* into a search engine. I rationalized that this did not constitute investigating. I was merely satisfying my own curiosity about what Cara was reporting with regard to Brea Ridge Pharmaceuticals and Fred's death.

I clicked on the link for the *West Side Messenger* home page and then typed Cara's name and "Brea Ridge" into the site's search engine. I sorted the results by "most recent." At the top of the list was the headline "Brea Ridge Reporter Latest Victim of Mystery Illness."

I opened the document. The report stated that "the illness which besieged Brea Ridge residents at a holiday party earlier this month has resurfaced." The article went on to hint that Brea Ridge might have an epidemic on its hands but that, fortunately, the good doctors at Brea Ridge Pharmaceuticals were available with their miracle cure, which enjoyed a 99 percent success rate.

So my paraphrasing is facetious. You still get the gist of

the article. The others were pretty much more of the same.

The first article dealt with the party and how a large number of guests became ill. Cara reported that one young man with a history of brain injury had gone into a coma and had not yet recovered. The article had a sidebar explaining campylobacter bacteria, how it is believed to be spread and how it is treated. Since that part was practical and not overly dramatizing, I figured someone else had written it and put it in at the suggestion of the editor.

Cara's article didn't mention where the party had taken place but stated that doctors involved in the development of a new drug treating the effects of campylobacter bacteria were on hand to take charge of the situation. She went on to sing the praises of Brea Ridge Pharmaceuticals and especially Dr. John Holloway.

I closed the article to read the next one and caught sight of the date again. The article ran the day after Fred died. Had Cara simply missed the deadline to amend her article and report Fred's death? Or had she sat on the information in order to provide herself another article with a dramatic "new" development the next day?

The next article was indeed relaying the "tragic" news of Fred's death and painting a maudlin word portrait of a community in mourning.

*Yet, none are more devastated by the news than the doctors of Brea Ridge Pharmaceuticals who so desperately tried to save this young man's life.*

My jaw literally dropped. *None* are more devastated? Tell that to Fred's mother.

My fingers itched to write a letter to the editor telling him or her and the entire Richmond area what a load of hot air Cara Logan is and what inaccurate articles she was writing. Oh, and that the "devastated doctors" are terrified Fred Duncan's mother is going to sue their pants off.

I unclenched my fists. While a letter to the *West Side Messenger* editor might be in order, I didn't need to do it tonight . . . in anger . . . via e-mail.

I closed that article and scrolled on down the page. Apparently, the only article Cara had written dealing with Brea Ridge other than detailing the current events surrounding the campylobacter outbreak was a fluff piece she'd done last October on supposed haunted sites in Brea Ridge, Abingdon and Bristol. That must've been in the days before her rise to super journalist.

Still disgusted about Cara, I typed the search engine URL into the destination box again. This time I searched for *Robert Franklin + retail management + Boone, North Carolina.* I wanted to see if Robby was as big a deal as his brother Steve had made him out to be. Maybe he was just a big deal in Steve's eyes.

Nope. Turns out, Robby was indeed a fairly big deal.

He was easy to find because of his status as Appalachian State University alum. Their alumni newsletter regularly sang his praises with an enthusiasm that had escaped Steve Franklin.

Robert Franklin was a successful manager of a chain of high-end jewelry stores. In addition to that, he was an accomplished pianist who sometimes gave free piano lessons at a local boys' and girls' organization. He was married to the lovely Patricia, nee Fuller, who was a teacher at a private school where the Franklins' two lovely daughters were in attendance. Lovely.

There was a photograph of Robby, and I had to begrudgingly admit that he, too, was lovely. Normally, I'd have called him a HUG—Hot Unavailable Guy—but knowing how unlovely he'd treated his brother and his brother's intended fiancé made me feel Robby didn't deserve the title.

I clicked out of the love fest to see if there were any other articles on Robert Franklin. There were some older pieces on his athletic achievements while at ASU. I didn't open those. Further accolades being heaped on Robby Franklin might make me gag on my hot cocoa.

There was another article, though, that did catch my eye. Two years ago, Robert Franklin had been arrested on suspicion of driving while intoxicated. The charge had been reduced to improper driving. Robby had paid a fine and had been given a suspended sentence.

A chill not even hot cocoa could dispel ran down my spine. Was there something Steve Franklin had failed to mention about his brother? It would make sense the other person involved in Fred's accident was never found because he lived somewhere other than Brea Ridge.

*

After a relatively sleepless night, I got up with one goal in mind—I was going to Save-A-Buck and asking Steve Franklin if his brother was the one who caused Fred's accident. I once again told myself this was not investigating, merely satisfying a curiosity. Besides, it had already been determined that Fred's accident had no bearing on his death so this could not even be remotely considered investigating Fred's death. Right? Right. And, I needed cake flour, confectioners' sugar, butter, eggs . . . the usual stuff.

When I got to Save-A-Buck, I went straight to Steve Franklin's office. His door was open, and he looked up and smiled when he saw me standing there.

"Good morning, Ms. Martin. Your candies have been a hit. Any chance you can make some more of them this weekend?"

"I'll see what I can do." I walked inside the office. "Have you got a minute?"

"Sure." He pushed his chair away from his desk and leaned back, clasping his hands behind his head.

I closed the door to his office. "I hope this won't have any bearing on our professional relationship, but I have to ask you this."

He raised a brow and I got the feeling he thought I was getting ready to ask him for a date or something. I spoke quickly.

"Did your brother cause Fred Duncan's accident last year?"

Everything dropped: Mr. Franklin's jaw, his clasped hands, and the foot he had resting on one knee. I was afraid he was going to fall completely out of his chair.

"A-are you . . .? W-what?" he asked.

I sat down in the chair by the door. "Last night I looked up your brother to see if he was really all that big a deal." I shrugged one shoulder. "China York had mentioned you and your brother had been estranged for several years over a girl, and I suppose I wanted to check him out so I could tell you I didn't think he was all that great."

Mr. Franklin rolled back up to his desk and stared down at his calendar. "We did go our separate ways. The girl was only part of it."

"I'm sorry."

He tilted his head. "Me, too. I really loved that girl . . . thought we had a future together, you know?"

"Still, sometimes people aren't who we think they are. And it's better to find that out sooner than later."

"Are we talking about your ex-husband now?"

"I don't know. I think I always knew he was a jerk, but I hoped maybe I could change him . . . or . . . something. Anyway, as the Big Dog shirt says, 'Better to have loved and lost than to live with a psycho the rest of your life.'"

"I guess."

"Anyway," I continued, "Robby's life looked pretty impressive at first glance. But then I saw he was arrested for DUI two years ago."

Mr. Franklin nodded slowly. "He was. And I have to admit when I heard about that, I gloated to myself over it a little. Robby's party-boy lifestyle was finally catching up to him. I thought it was high time. But then the charge was reduced and, as always, Robby walked away smelling like a lavender sachet in a drawer full of expensive lingerie."

"Okay, thanks for putting that strange analogy in my head. Do you think he's the person responsible for Fred's accident?"

"Why do you ask?" He chewed on the inside of his cheek.

"I'm curious, that's all. If you think he is but never confronted him, then why not? Here is finally your chance to point a finger at your brother and say, 'I know what you did, and you're going to make it right. For once in your life, you're going to do the responsible thing.' If you did confront him when it happened and he denied it, then at least you confronted him. You know you did the right thing."

He barked out a laugh. "It seems I always do the right thing where Robby is concerned. In this case, I asked Mom how Robby was when he was there and if he'd been drinking. Mom got angry with me and ordered me out of her house."

"What about Robby? Did you ask him?"

"No. We weren't speaking at all . . . hadn't in years." He sighed, took off his glasses and rubbed his eyes. "If anyone was responsible for Fred's accident, it was me. I'm the one who sent him over there with Mom's flowers. I'm the one who didn't have the guts to face my brother on our mother's birthday. I'm the reason Fred Duncan is dead."

"That's not true. You had no way of knowing Fred would be in an accident that afternoon."

"It doesn't matter. I'm the one who should've been on that road. It should've been me in that accident . . . not Fred."

"Still, Mr. Franklin, if you believe your brother caused that accident—"

"I don't, all right? When Mom calmed down a week or so later, she called and told me she knew I was only concerned about Robby when I'd asked if he'd been drinking . . . that she realized I wanted to protect him in case he was responsible for Fred's accident." He scoffed. "Yeah, sure, Mom. Anyway, she said he'd been in court-ordered alcohol rehab and had been sober for over a year. I let it go after that." He dropped his head into his hands again. "I'm so sorry . . . so sorry about Fred. I never meant for any of this to happen."

"Mr. Franklin, I think you should know neither Fred's accident nor his brain injury had any bearing whatsoever on his death . . . the hospital confirmed that to his cousin Fran. She's helping me cater Belinda Fremont's party."

He slid his hands down his tear-streaked face and looked at me. "Are you just telling me that to make me feel better?"

"No. It's the truth. I promise."

"Thank you. It still doesn't erase the guilt I feel over

causing Fred to be on that road in the first place, but it does make me feel that maybe I'm not responsible for his death. I know I acted like a complete jerk after he died, but I . . . I guess the only way to deal with it was to pretend to other people that it didn't matter. But it did, Daphne."

"I know." I stood. "I'll see about getting your customers some more candy here by Monday morning." I figured I could drop it off on the way to pick up Lucas and Leslie.

"Thank you."

I opened the door and went back to the front of the store for a shopping cart. As I gathered the items I needed, I rehashed my conversation with Mr. Franklin. His mother initially became angry over his questions about Robby. Isn't it possible she knew Robby was drinking and was covering for him in order to protect him? Mr. Franklin had made it clear his mother would do anything for Robby. I didn't have a doubt in my mind she'd cover for him if he was guilty of another DUI plus facing charges of leaving the scene of an accident which resulted in injury to another party. If Robby Franklin did cause Fred's accident, the statute of limitations would not start to run until his actions were confirmed . . . which may be never . . . but could be as soon as Steve Franklin got the nerve to confront his brother.

*

When I arrived home and put my groceries away, I checked the answering machine. There was a message from Dr. Broadstreet.

"Daphne, this is Quentin Broadstreet of Brea Ridge Pharmaceuticals. My wife Dorothy and I would like to meet with you here in my office at noon today. If you cannot make our appointment, then please call my receptionist and leave me a message to that effect. Otherwise, Dorothy and I will see you at noon."

The machine beeped signaling the end of the message.

I looked at the clock. I had a couple hours before I had to leave to meet with the Broadstreets. That didn't give me much time to bake or decorate. Instead, I decided to check my email, take a look at my website to see how much traffic it was generating and piddle away a few minutes.

I turned on the computer, logged onto the Internet and checked my mail. It was mostly junk. Some subject lines gave me the happy news that I'd won a lottery I'd never even entered, while others were downright offensive. I deleted them all.

I glanced over my to-do list. Instead of checking anything off, I added four items.

Sighing, I visited my website statistics page. Visits to the site were down for the second straight week in a row. Joy.

I played a game of solitaire and lost. Minesweeper? Lost that game four times.

I was not enjoying my computer time. Plus, while I was hoping the Broadstreets wanted to hire me, Dr. Broadstreet's detailed message had not mentioned anything pertaining to that fact, so I really didn't know what they wanted.

The site address for *West Side Messenger* was still in my browser history, so I opened the page to see if Cara had reported anything new about her misadventures in "quaint" Brea Ridge. There was nothing new, so I decided to read her fluff piece on local hauntings. I wanted to see if the woman could write an article to save her life that wasn't biased in some way.

I double clicked the article. When it came up on the screen, the first thing that struck me was the date. It was the day after Fred Duncan's car accident. The second thing was that the first haunting on her list was the old mill on Fox Hollow Road, complete with recent photographs.

## Chapter Fifteen

I touched up my makeup and put on a nicer sweater before going to Brea Ridge Pharmaceuticals to meet with Dr. Broadstreet and his wife. I took my portfolio and some business cards in case the meeting was—as I expected and hoped—about a cake or some other baked goods they wanted me to prepare. Maybe they were even going the Belinda Fremont route and wanted me to cater an entire party.

When I arrived at Brea Ridge Pharmaceuticals and was told I could go on back to Dr. Broadstreet's office, I saw that Connie had been dead on in her description of Mrs. Broadstreet. The song *Aquarius* started going through my mind the instant I saw her. She had long, graying brown hair. Two skinny braids adorned with beads framed her face. She wore little round John Lennon-style glasses, a tie-dyed t-shirt and faded bell-bottomed jeans. And she definitely was skinny. I felt that if she stood up and turned sideways, she might disappear.

I extended my hand in greeting. "Hi, I'm Daphne Martin."

She shook my hand gently and smiled. "It's a pleasure to meet you. My husband has been raving about your oatmeal bread. I have to admit, I don't remember much about your cake. The hours following that party are a blur." Her eyes darted from me to her husband and back.

"I can imagine."

"Do you have recipes for vegan cakes?" she asked.

"I do. I have a chocolate cake recipe that uses applesauce rather than oil and eggs, and I have recipes for lemon poppy seed, carrot, banana and even rum cake."

Mrs. Broadstreet smiled at her husband. "Quent, I've found my baker."

Dr. Broadstreet nodded. "I told you so."

"He loves to tell me that," she said to me.

"All men love to tell their wives 'I told you so'. . . probably because it's such a rare occasion," I said.

She laughed. "Wonderful. When can I sample some of your cakes?"

"I can prepare a sampler for you this weekend, and I can bring it back here on Tuesday, if you'd like."

"Wonderful. That way both Quentin and I can choose our favorites."

I wrote this information down in my portfolio and handed Mrs. Broadstreet a business card. I turned to Dr. Broadstreet. "Doctor, do you mind if I ask you a question?"

"Not at all," he said.

"I know Mrs. Broadstreet prepared food for the Christmas party, as did I," I said, "but since none of the food contained any of the campylobacter bacteria, where did it come from?"

Dr. Broadstreet stroked his beard. "Your guess is as good as anyone's, Ms. Martin."

"I was so afraid I'd bought something contaminated from the health food store," Mrs. Broadstreet said. "I buy organic, and I'm so cautious about buying foods that have been sprayed with pesticides or other chemicals." She shook her head. "I didn't think it was in the food, but, you know, that is the usual presumption. I was relieved when the police report came back."

"So was I," I said. "Is there any of the bacteria kept here at the lab?"

"Oh, sure," Dr. Broadstreet said. "Among other things. There are all sorts of bacteria in our labs. That's how we make drugs to combat them."

Mrs. Broadstreet shuddered.

I shared her distaste but tried not to be as obvious. "Of course. I just can't imagine how that particular bacterium infected various people at the party. It had to be one of the guests, didn't it?"

"Not necessarily," Dr. Broadstreet said. "Why would you think so?"

"Because I heard—I believe from Cara Logan—that if the bacterium got on someone's hands, they would get sick, too. It would be impossible to infect someone without infecting yourself. Isn't that right?"

"Yes and no," he said. "You can handle the bacterium with gloves."

"But someone wearing latex gloves contaminating . . . *something* . . . at the party would certainly have aroused suspicion," Mrs. Broadstreet said. "And I saw nothing out of the ordinary."

Dr. Broadstreet grinned at his wife. "Maybe the contaminator was wearing invisible gloves."

I gaped. *Invisible gloves.* I remembered my ex-husband smearing on a protective hand coating before working on his vintage car. "Is that possible?"

"I was joking, Ms. Martin."

"I know, but is there something a person could use to coat his hands that would protect him from the bacterium but allow him to spread it to others? Perhaps through touching them . . . like shaking hands?"

Dr. Broadstreet's smile faded. "Like silicone." He nodded. "There are products made to protect one's hands . . . ."

"But who would do such a thing?" Mrs. Broadstreet asked.

I remembered Cara touching Ben's hand at the restaurant. Shortly afterwards, he became ill. "I think I know."

"Well, please, tell us," Dr. Broadstreet said.

"I respectfully request your patience with me," I said. "I'd like to speak with her before I make any accusations."

"Her?" he asked.

"Um . . . if you'll excuse me," I said. "I'll see you both on Tuesday. Shall we say noon again?"

"Noon will be fine," Mrs. Broadstreet said.

I went back out to Helen, the receptionist. "Have you seen Cara Logan here today?"

"I have. She came and picked Dr. Holloway up for lunch."

"Do you know when they'll be back?"

"No idea, hon. You're welcome to wait, but I have no idea how long they'll be. Sometimes I think they have those three martini lunches out at his place on Fox Hollow Road." Helen snickered. "At least, Dr. Holloway is in a good mood when they get back."

I nodded. "In that case, I don't believe I'll wait."

"I don't blame you. Want to leave a message?"

"No. I'll try to give Ms. Logan a call later."

I went outside and got into my car. I called Ben, but my call went straight to voice mail. He must be at lunch, too. I left a message. "Ben, it's me. I believe I know who made all the people sick at the party . . . and you, too, for that matter. It was Cara. I even know how she did it. Call me."

*

On a hunch, when I pulled out of the Brea Ridge Pharmaceuticals parking lot, I found myself turning the Mini Cooper in the direction of Fox Hollow Road.

*What am I doing? Am I insane? This definitely crosses from curiosity over into full-blown investigating.*

*Or does it? I'm just doing a drive by. Once again, merely satisfying my curiosity. I wouldn't know Dr. Holloway's house if I saw it. I have no idea what either he or Cara drives.*

*Besides that, I can't be sure either of them caused Fred Duncan's accident a year ago, and I have no proof that Cara caused the people at the Christmas party to get sick.*

And yet when I got there, I found myself pulling onto Fox Hollow Road . . . and driving slowly.

Most of the houses on this road had obviously been around for years. While some had updates, I could tell they had been constructed back in the late sixties or early seventies and, judging by their continuity, by the same developer. They were single-story ranch style houses. I could even tell when more of the land was sold to make way for new houses later on. These houses were split-level homes and duplexes. A couple of the duplexes had been modified to become one home, but I could see where there had once been two units to the houses.

Then I rounded a curve and saw the McMansion. Oh, no, that hadn't been there for thirty or forty years. It looked like somewhere a doctor might live. Dark red brick went on for what seemed like miles in both directions. There was no porch—no one living in this home had time to relax. Three super-sized windows with rounded tops dominated the second floor of the house, and an enormous chandelier was visible even from the road. The first floor had a white door encased by narrow windows and a couple picture windows whose interior views were concealed by shades. A BMW sat in the driveway. A black BMW sedan.

Anyone with any sense would have turned around—preferably in someone else's driveway—and gone home. I plead a stress-induced insanity with a possible blackout situation; because the next thing, I knew, I was parked in the McDriveway.

There was time to back out, I know, but see the above insanity/blackout defense. Because, once again, the next thing I knew, I was ringing—you guessed it—the McDoorbell.

Dr. Holloway came to the door. His hair was messed up and his glasses were a tad askew. I was interrupting something. Probably making out, but who knows? Cara might have been trying to McMurder him. I was having serious suspicions about her.

"Hello, Daphne. What are you doing here?"

I smiled; but it was so fake it made my face hurt, so I quit. *So what now? Do I try to sell the doctor a cake? Do I tell him I'm looking for Cara? Say I'm investigating Fred Duncan's accident which happened over a year ago and is no longer relevant anyway because the young man is dead?* Once again, see insanity/blackout defense. "Dr. Holloway, I think Cara is responsible for the people at your party getting sick."

"What?" he asked.

"Who's there?" Cara asked, coming to the door carrying a glass of wine. "Daphne? I thought that was your voice I heard. What's going on? Are you making a move on my boyfriend right in front of me now?"

"Darling, Daphne is making a serious accusation against you," Dr. Holloway said, "and I think she might want to reconsider it."

"You're right," I said, "I might. But first I'd like to speak with the two of you."

Dr. Holloway stood aside and allowed me entrance into the stone foyer. There was a staircase to the right and the living room to the left. I stepped onto the plush beige carpet of the living room and turned back to look at Cara and Dr. Holloway. He closed the door and began walking toward me. I backed further into the living room. When I felt a coffee table at my calves, I turned and sat down on the brown leather sofa.

"You have a lovely home," I said.

"Thank you. Please say what you came here to say so Cara and I can finish our lunch." Neither he nor Cara sat.

"All right. I apologize if I'm off track or out of line here, but I was at your office earlier today meeting with Dr. Broadstreet and his wife, Dorothy. We started talking about how someone might have infected people with the virus other than putting it in the food."

"I don't see how this involves me," Cara said, flipping her tousled hair over her shoulder.

"Have you ever heard of a product favored by automotive workers, artists and manufacturers which coats their hands so their skin will come clean and won't absorb the chemicals they're working with?" I asked.

When they shared a glance, I knew I was right. I also knew I was in trouble. I was in the McMansion with the shades drawn on a godforsaken strip of road few people traveled, and no one had a clue as to where I was.

"You probably don't," I said, rising to my feet. "It was a silly assumption. But, when Ben got sick after Cara touched his hand at the restaurant, I just . . . well, I guess I jumped to conclusions. If that was an Olympic event—jumping to conclusions—I could probably be a gold medalist!" I gave a little laugh. "Sorry I interrupted your . . . your lunch." I jabbed my thumb toward the door. "I'll be on my way."

Cara stepped closer to me. "I don't believe you will. Your accusations—no matter how unfounded—could ruin John and me."

"Well, since you two are the only people I told, there's no need to worry about it, right? I mean, are you planning to do an article about it?"

"No, and neither is Benny."

"Oh, is that what you're afraid of?" I asked. "That you've been scooped?" I shook my head. "No, not at all. Ben always verifies the truth of his articles before they're printed." I stared at Cara. "As I'm sure you do."

"Of course."

"Besides," I said, "you'd never intentionally cause John or his company harm, would you, Cara?"

She looked at him. "No. You know I wouldn't."

"I mean good grief, you covered up the accident involving Fred Duncan a year ago and didn't even report it. Instead you gave the paper a fluff piece on hauntings."

"The piece on hauntings is what I was sent to do," Cara said, peering from me to Dr. Holloway. "I didn't know Fred Duncan or anyone else would be on the road that day, I swear. It was an odd time of day, I was on my way to the mill . . . ."

"So you didn't cover for Dr. Holloway," I said. "You caused the accident and covered up for yourself."

"I never said that!" she cried.

Dr. Holloway swallowed convulsively. "You said you had nothing to do with Fred Duncan's car accident."

"I didn't." She glared at me. "She's the one who said I did."

"But I asked you that night because it happened shortly after you left here," he said, "and you said it wasn't you. I didn't care if it was—I'd have helped you get out of it or get a reduced sentence or something—but you swore it wasn't you."

"And I just told you again it wasn't me, John!" She placed her hands on her hips. "Who are you going to believe? Me or her?"

"You claimed you didn't even know Fred Duncan," he continued mechanically. "That's what you said after he became sick. 'How was I supposed to know he was the one with the brain injury?' you asked me when he didn't get better." He slowly blinked and turned his head toward Cara.

An image of a turtle flashed through my mind. But

suddenly, he turned into a snapping turtle.

"Your lies have cost me my career!" he shouted, moving toward her. "How could I be such a fool? She might bend the truth a little with others, I thought, but she'd never lie to me. She loves me." He shook his head. "And I loved you."

Cara started to cry. "Don't, John. Everything is fine. We can spin this."

"That's always your answer, isn't it?" he asked. "'We can spin this. I'll make the reporter sick, you can make him better, and you'll be a hero again. Fred's death was really no big deal.' And I went along with it."

"And it worked," she said. "I went on TV, people started calling the office. It's going fine. As long as we don't let *her* ruin it all now. Let's just get rid of her and be done with it."

"Oh, yeah, Cara, let's do that. Let's add premeditated murder to everything else. At this point, my career might be sunk, but I'm not in prison. And I'm not going." He took a long deep breath. "I'm calling 9-1-1."

Cara's eyes widened. "No! You can't!" Then her eyes narrowed. "You will not pin this whole thing on me, John Holloway. I'll swear up and down that you planned the entire thing and that you knew I caused Fred Duncan to wreck last year and didn't say anything and that you gave me the bacterium to infect Ben Jacobs even after you knew someone had died from it. Now what are you gonna do?"

He calmly picked up the phone. "The right thing . . . for once."

She slapped the phone out of his hand and turned on me. "You! This is all your fault!" She picked up a lamp with a large terra cotta base and hurled it at my head.

I ducked, and the lamp smashed against the picture window directly behind me. At the sound of breaking glass, I was fairly certain both the window and the lamp had shattered, but I didn't dare turn to look. I was too busy keeping an eye on Cara and wondering what she was going to do next.

Dr. Holloway grabbed her from behind. She elbowed him in the stomach; and when he bent forward, she hit him in the face with the back of her fist. That was a move I, too, had learned in self-defense class.

"This isn't over!" she cried before running out the front door.

I stood where I was, still unsure the coast was clear. When I heard the BMW roar out of the McDriveway, I decided to hazard a peep out the window. She was leaving. I wouldn't have been very surprised if she'd driven the BMW through the house. I'm guessing only her sense of self-preservation kept her from doing so.

I picked up the phone which was lying on the carpet in front of John Holloway. "I'll go ahead and call 9-1-1."

After making the call, I looked at Dr. Holloway. His glasses weren't broken, but I was afraid his nose might be.

"You really should have that looked about," I said.

He merely turned and climbed the steps.

I went outside and locked myself in the Mini Cooper until Officer McAfee arrived.

*

As I drove home, I was struck by the irony of Cara fleeing the scene of one crime on Fox Hollow Road only to be caught there in another crime over a year later. Of course, I didn't stick around for the capture; but Officer McAfee assured me she'd be caught before she got out of Brea Ridge.

I pulled into the driveway, happy this mess had been resolved. The first thing I noticed when I stepped onto my walkway was that Sparrow was at the edge of the porch. She looked twice her normal size. I realized that was because her hair was standing up.

"What's the matter, Sparrow?" I asked softly.

She was close to the side door where I'd normally go in. I felt we'd been making progress in our relationship, but I wasn't dumb enough to test it yet. If something had scared her, she might scratch me if I reached out to her.

I decided to go through the front door and check on her after I had lunch. I looked through my key ring for the front door key as I went around to the front. Before I could unlock the door, I heard a crash on the side porch followed by Sparrow's yowl.

I hurried back to see what had happened. Cara was standing behind an overturned trash can wielding a tire iron. Sparrow was nowhere in sight.

"If you hurt my cat," I said, "so help me, I'll—"

"You're not calling the shots here!" she screamed. She kicked the trash can out of her way and advanced slowly toward me.

"The police are looking for you, and they'll be here any minute."

With a guttural growl of fury, she ran toward me with the tire iron over her head ready to strike. "If I go, I'm taking you with me. You ruined everything!"

I dropped my purse and keys onto the porch. When Cara got close enough, I grabbed the wrist of the hand with the tire iron. Cara retaliated by pulling my hair. That's when I head butted her. Afterwards, I couldn't believe I did it. But my head was already hurting from the hair pulling, so I just went Keifer Sutherland on her.

When my head slammed into her nose, she dropped my hair and the tire iron. The tire iron barely missed my shoulder and landed with a clang on the porch. I grasped her other wrist to keep her from picking something else up. Her nose was bleeding pretty badly, though, and I think most of the fight had gone out of her.

I heard a car pull into my driveway. I didn't dare look to see who it was, but I desperately hoped it was not John Holloway coming to help Cara.

"O M G!" Fran yelled as she eased up beside me. "Are you okay?"

"Speak in words, rather than letters," I said. "You've been texting too much. Call 9-1-1, would you please?"

"Sure."

I glanced at her from the corner of my eye. Her eyes were huge—or as Leslie would say, ginormous. "Everything's all right."

## Chapter Sixteen

Officer McAfee arrived and took custody of Cara within minutes of Fran's call. I was thrilled; my arms were exhausted. They found Cara's car one street over from mine.

Fran was really impressed I could "kick butt." I told her that taking self-defense lessons from a retired Marine living in my apartment building in Tennessee had paid off enormously. She'd come to bake, but I suggested we take the day off and start fresh tomorrow morning.

Myra had been out Christmas shopping, so she was none the wiser . . . yet. Neither was Violet. But in a town the size of Brea Ridge, word travels fast; and I knew I'd have to answer a lot of questions before long.

After the police and Fran had left, I picked up my purse and keys and took them into the house. I came back outside, sat on the step and called for Sparrow. She didn't come. I put my head on my knees, closed my eyes and waited. When everything was quiet, I felt Sparrow brush against me. I looked down and saw that she appeared to be fine. I stroked her gently and saw that she had only been scared, not hurt.

Against my better judgment, I picked her up. She didn't particularly care for it, but she tolerated a quick hug. Then I got up, opened the door, and she went inside.

When Ben arrived about an hour later, Sparrow and I were sitting on the kitchen floor. She was eating a trout China York had brought her. China had heard about my ordeal over the scanner. She'd brought muffins for me, and a trout for the cat. Seriously, she brought a trout.

Ben could see us through the open door, so he didn't knock. Sparrow looked up, saw Ben and darted under the kitchen table.

I got up and opened the door. "Hi."

He stepped inside and crushed me to him. "Are you okay?" He held me at arm's length to look me over.

"I'm fine, Ben. Let me wash the trout off my hands, and I'll join you in the living room."

When I got to the living room, Ben was sitting on the sofa looking at the picture Fred had drawn. I sat beside him, and he put his arm around me.

"That's new," he said, nodding toward the picture.

"Mm-hm. Fred Duncan drew it. His mom had it matted and framed for me."

"It's beautiful."

"Thanks." I sighed and rested my head against his shoulder. "I hope Violet will still let me take Lucas and Leslie shopping on Monday. She was against me investigating Fred's death from the very start, and I promised her all along I'd stay out of it."

"You can't help it," Ben said. "You're nosy."

"Gee, you say the sweetest things."

He laughed. "I'm kidding."

"As if."

"Besides, why wouldn't Violet let you take the kids shopping?" he asked. "You're like Lara Croft or something. They'd have their own personal bodyguard."

"You so exaggerate. I just don't want her mad at me. I'd hate to have to live like Steve Franklin and his brother."

"What about Steve Franklin and his brother?"

"They haven't spoken in years," I said. "Mainly because Steve's brother Robby stole Steve's girlfriend, dated her for a few days and then dumped her."

"I remember Robby Franklin," Ben said. "He was a jerk. Still, it doesn't sound as if the girl was worth ruining a relationship over. What happened to her?"

"She left town. And, no, it doesn't sound like she was the best girl in the world, but Steve Franklin really loved her. He was heartbroken when she left, and he never found anyone to fill that void. Can you imagine that?" I looked up at Ben.

"Yeah, actually, I can." He smiled. "Maybe Steve will luck up and his girl will come home, too."

## THE END

*Dead Pan*

# Recipes
Many thanks to Holly Clegg, author, the *trim&Terrific*
cookbooks

## Apple, Brie, and Brown Sugar Pizza

Oh my goodness....this is the absolute best!! Imagine a thin
crisp crust topped with rich, creamy Brie and cinnamon apples.
This pizza could be served for brunch, a snack or a light
dessert. It is hard to beat or resist hot out of the oven—even a
house full of 20 year old boys were grabbing for another piece.
Miniature pizza crusts are a fun way to serve these pizzas.
Makes 8 slices

1 (13.8-ounce) can refrigerated pizza crust
4 ounces Brie, rind removed and thinly sliced
1 large baking apple, peeled, cored, and thinly sliced
3 tablespoons chopped pecans
3 tablespoons light brown sugar
1/2 teaspoon ground cinnamon

1 Preheat oven 450°F.
2. On top of pizza crust, arrange Brie and apple slices
concentrically around crust. In small bowl, mix together
remaining ingredients, sprinkle over apples.
3. Bake 10–12 minutes or until cheese is melted and apples are
tender. Slice, serve.

**Nutritional information per serving:**
Calories 193, Calories from fat (%) 33, Fat (g) 7, Saturated Fat
(g) 3, Cholesterol (mg) 14, Sodium (mg) 328, Carbohydrate (g)
26, Dietary Fiber (g) 1, Sugars (g) 10, Protein (g) 6, Diabetic
Exchanges: 1 1/2 starch, 1 medium-fat meat

Terrific Tidbit: I prefer Granny Smith apples as they are tart and compliment the Brie. Any large, thin round, unbaked pizza crust may be used.

## Sweet Potato Praline Coffee Cake

Hot out of the oven, this scrumptious, melt-in-your mouth, eye-appealing recipe is hard to beat and best of all, it tastes equally as good after being frozen. The sensational praline topping glazes the top making every bite a yummy one. A personal favorite.

Makes 12 servings

4 tablespoons butter
2/3 cup plus 3 tablespoons light brown sugar, divided
2 tablespoons light corn syrup
1/2 cup chopped pecans
2 1/2 cups biscuit baking mix
1 (15-ounce) can sweet potatoes (yams), drained and mashed or
1 cup mashed sweet
potatoes
1/3 cup skim milk
1/4 cup dried cranberries

1. Preheat oven to 400° F. In 9x9x-2 square nonstick baking pan, melt butter in oven. Stir in 2/3 cup brown sugar and corn syrup; spread evenly in pan. Sprinkle with pecans.
2. In large mixing bowl, beat together biscuit baking mix, sweet potatoes, and milk until dough forms a ball.
3. Turn dough onto a surface dusted with baking mix, knead several times and roll or pat into 12-inch rectangle. Sprinkle with remaining 3 tablespoons brown sugar and cranberries.
4. Roll up dough jellyroll style from longer side. Cut crosswise into one-inch pieces and arrange sitting on top of pecan mixture in pan. The dough will spread when baking.

5. Bake 25 - 30 minutes or until golden brown. Immediately turn upside down onto serving plate.

To Prepare and Eat Now: Eat when ready.

To Freeze: Cool to room temperature, wrap, label and freeze.

To Serve: Thaw to room temperature and serve. The coffee cake may be reheated in the oven at 350° F. or in the microwave.

## Nutrition information per serving:
Calories 276, Protein (g) 2, Carbohydrate (g) 43, Fat (g) 11, Calories from Fat (%) 36, Saturated Fat (g) 4, Dietary Fiber (g) 1, Cholesterol (mg) 10, Sodium (mg) 360, Diabetic Exchanges: 3 starch, 2 fat

*Dead Pan*

Meet Daphne Martin
MURDER TAKES THE CAKE
Book One
The Daphne Martin Cake Decorating Mysteries
Gayle Trent
Trade Paperback 14.95
Ebook at Fictionwise.com

Excerpt

## CHAPTER ONE

"Mrs. Watson?" I called, banging on the door again. I glanced up at the ever-blackening clouds. Although I had Mrs. Watson's cake in a box, it would be my luck to get caught in a downpour with it. This was my third attempt to please her, and I couldn't afford another mistake on the amount she was paying me. Whoever said "the customer is always right" had obviously never dealt with Yodel Watson.

I heard something from inside the house and pressed my ear against the door. A vision of my falling into the living room and dropping the cake when Mrs. Watson flung open the door made me rethink that decision.

"Mrs. Watson?" I called again.

"Come in! It's open! Come in!"

I tried the knob and the door was indeed unlocked. I stepped inside but couldn't see Mrs. Watson. "It's me—Daphne Martin. I'm here with your cake."

"Come in! It's open!"

"I am in, Mrs. Watson. Where are you?"

"It's open!"

"I know! I—" Gritting my teeth, I walked through the living room and placed the cake on the kitchen table. A quick glance around the kitchen told me Mrs. Watson wasn't in there either.

"It's open!"

Man, could this lady get on your nerves. I decided to follow the voice. It came from my left, so I eased down the hallway.

"Mrs. Watson?"

On my right, there was a den. I poked my head inside.

"Come in!"

I turned toward the voice. A gray parrot was sitting on its perch inside its cage.

"It's open!" the bird squawked.

"I noticed." *Great. She's probably not home, and I'll get arrested for breaking and entering . . . though technically, I didn't break . . .*

It was then I saw Mrs. Watson lying on the sofa in a faded navy robe. There was a plaid blanket over her legs. She appeared to be sleeping, but I'd heard the parrot calling when I was outside. No way could Mrs. Watson be in the same room and sleep through that racket.

I stepped closer. "Are you okay?" Her pallor told me she was not okay. Then the foul odor hit me.

I backed away and took my cell phone out of my purse. "I'm calling 9-1-1, Mrs. Watson. Everything's gonna be all right." I don't know if I was trying to reassure her or myself.

*Everything's gonna be all right.* I'd been telling myself that for the past month.

I lingered in the doorway in case Mrs. Watson would wake up and need something before the EMTs arrived.

I turned forty this year. Forty seems to be a sobering age for every woman, but it hit me especially hard. When most women get to be my age, they at least have some bragging rights: successful career, happy marriage, beautiful children, nice home. I had none of the above. My so-called bragging rights included a failed marriage, a dingy apartment, and twenty years' service in a dead-end job. Cue violins.

When my sister Violet called and told me about a "charming little house" for sale near her neighborhood, I jumped at the chance to leave all the dead ends of middle

Tennessee and come home to southwest Virginia. Surely, something better awaited me here.

So far, I'd moved into my house—which I recently learned came with a one-eyed stray cat—and started a cake decorating business. A great deal of my time had involved coming up with a name, a logo, getting business cards made up, setting up a web site and other "fun" administrative duties. The cake and cupcakes I'd made for my niece and nephew to take to school on Halloween had been a hit, though, and had led to some nice word-of-mouth advertising and a couple orders. Leslie's puppy dog cake and Lucas' black cat cupcakes were the first additions to my web site's gallery.

Sadly, my first customer had been Yodel Watson. She'd considered herself a world-class baker in her hey-day, but no longer had the time or desire to engage in "such foolishness."

"I want you to make me a cake for my Thanksgiving dinner," she'd said. "Nothing too gaudy. I want my family to think I made it myself."

My first two attempts had been refused: the first cake was too fancy; the second was too plain. I'd been hoping—*praying*—third time would be the charm. Now the laboriously prepared spice cake with cream cheese frosting decorated with orange and red satin ribbons for a bottom border and a red apple arranged in a flower petal pattern on top was on Mrs. Watson's kitchen table. Mrs. Watson herself was lying on her den sofa as deflated as a December jack-o-lantern. Oh, yeah, things were looking up.

I was startled out of my reverie by a sharp rap.

"EMT!"

"Come in! It's open!" the bird called.

I hurried to the living room to open the door, and two men with a stretcher brushed past me.

"Where's the patient?" one asked.

"Back here." I led the way to the den, and then got out of the way.

"Come in!"

I moved next to the bird cage. "Don't you ever shut up?

This is serious."

"I'll say," agreed one of the EMTs. "Are you the next of kin?"

"Excuse me?" My hand flew to my throat. "She's dead?"

"Yes, ma'am. Are you related to her?"

While the one EMT was questioning me, the other was on the radio asking dispatch to send the police and the coroner.

"I don't know anything," I said. "I just brought the cake."

*

After calling in the reinforcements, the EMT's sent me back to the living room. They didn't get any argument from me. I sat down on the edge of a burgundy wingback chair and studied the room.

It was a formal living room; and on my previous visits, I'd only been just inside the front door. This room was a far cry from the den. The den was lived in. *Ugh. Bad choice of words.*

This room seemed as sterile as an operating room. There was an elaborate Oriental rug over beige carpet, a pale blue sofa, a curio cabinet with all sorts of expensive-looking knick-knacks. Unlike the den, this room was spotless.

Except for that.

Near my right foot was a small yellow stain. Parrot pee, I supposed. Still, even if Mrs. Watson had allowed the bird outside its cage, I'd have thought this room would've been off limits.

Maybe that's what killed her. Maybe she came in here and saw bird pee in her perfect room and had a heart attack. Then she returned to the den to collapse so as not to further contaminate the room.

Funny thing, though; I didn't even know Mrs. Watson had a bird until today.

"Ms. Martin?"

I looked up. It was one of the deputies.

"Yes?"

"I'm Officer Hayden, and I need to ask you some questions."

"Um . . . sure." This guy looked young enough to be my

son—scratch that, *nephew*—and he still made me nervous.

"Tell me about your arrival, ma'am."

Ma'am. Like I was seventy. Of course, when you're twelve, everybody looks old.

I cleared my throat. "I, uh, knocked on the door, and someone told me to come in. I thought it was Mrs. Watson, so I opened the door and came on inside." I pointed toward the kitchen table. "I'm Daphne of Daphne's Delectable Cakes." I patted my pockets for my business card holder, but realized I must have left it in the car. "I brought the cake."

Officer Hayden took out a notepad. "Let me get this straight. Someone else was here when you arrived?"

"No . . . no, it was the bird. The bird hollered and told me to come in."

He closed his eyes and pinched the bridge of his nose.

"I thought it was her, though." *Please, God, don't let me get arrested.* "It told me the door was open, and it *was.*"

Officer Hayden opened his eyes.

Never being one to know when to shut up, I reiterated, "I just brought the cake."

\*

About an hour later, I pulled into my driveway. I didn't make it to the front door before I heard my next-door-neighbor calling me.

"Hello, Daphne! I see you're bringing home another cake."

"Afraid so."

She beat me to the porch. For a woman in her sixties, Myra Jenkins was pretty quick. "What was wrong with this one?"

I handed Myra the cake and unlocked the door. "Um . . . she didn't say."

"She didn't say?" Myra wiped her feet on the mat and followed me inside.

I dropped my purse onto the table by the door. I let Myra hang onto the cake. She'd kept the other two rejects. I figured she'd take this one, too.

I went into the kitchen and took two diet sodas from the fridge. I handed Myra a soda, popped the top on the other, and took a long drink before dropping into a chair.

"This is beautiful," Myra said, after opening the cake box and peering inside. "What kind of cake is it?"

"Spice. The icing is cream cheese."

Myra ran her finger through the frosting on the side of the cake and licked her finger. "Mmm, this is out of this world. You know the Save-A-Buck sometimes takes baked goods on commission, don't you?"

"No, I didn't know that."

She nodded. "They don't keep a bakery staff, so they sometimes buy cakes, cookies, doughnuts—stuff like that—from the locals and sell them in their store."

"I'll definitely look into that."

"You should." She put the lid down on the box. "Are you going to take this one?"

"No," I said, thinking her poking the side had already nullified that possibility. "Why don't you take it?"

"Thank you. I believe I'll serve this one and the white one with the raspberry filling for Thanksgiving and save the chocolate one for Christmas." She smiled. "Do I owe you anything?"

"Yes. Good publicity. Sing my praises to the church group, the quilting circle, the library group and any other social cause you're participating in."

"Will do, honey. Will do."

"Um . . . how well do you know Yodel Watson?" I asked.

Myra pulled out a chair and sat down. "About as well as anybody in this town, I reckon. Why?"

"She . . . " I sighed. "She's dead."

She gasped. "What happened? Car wreck? You know, she drives the awfulest car I've ever seen. All the tires are bald, the—"

"It wasn't a car wreck," I interrupted. "When I went to her house, I thought she told me to come in, so—"

"Banjo."

"I beg your pardon?"

"It was probably Yodel's bird Banjo tellin' you to come in."

"Right. It was. So, uh, I went in and . . . and found Mrs. Watson in the den."

"And she was dead?"

I nodded.

"Was she naked?"

"No! She had on a robe and was covered with a blanket. Why would you think she was naked?"

Myra shrugged. "When people find dead bodies in the movies, the bodies are usually naked." She opened her soda. "So what happened?"

"I don't know. Since there was no obvious cause of death, she's being sent for an autopsy."

"Were there any opened envelopes lying around? Maybe somebody sent Yodel some of that *amtrax* stuff."

"I don't think it was anthrax," I corrected. "I figure she had a heart attack or an aneurysm or something."

"Don't be too sure."

"Why do you say that?"

"Because Yodel was mean." Myra took a drink of her soda. "Heck, you know that."

I shook my head and tried to steer the conversation away from murder. "Who'd name their daughter Yodel?"

"Oh, honey."

In the short time I've lived here, I've already learned that when Myra Jenkins says *Oh, honey,* you're in for a story.

"The Watsons yearned to follow in the Carter family's footsteps," she said. "You know, those famous singers. Yodel's sisters were Melody and Harmony, and her brother was Guitar. Guitar Refrain Watson—Tar, for short."

I nearly spit diet soda across the table. "You're kidding."

"No, honey, I'm not. Trouble was, nary a one of them Watsons had any talent. When my daughter was little, she'd clap her hands over her ears and make the most awful faces if we happened to sit behind them in church. Just about anybody can sing that 'Praise God From Whom All Blessings Flow' song they sing while takin' the offering plates back up to the alter, but the Watsons couldn't. And the worst part was, every one of them sang out loud and proud. Loud, proud, off-key and tone deaf." She smiled. "I have to admit, though, the congregation as a whole said a lot more silent prayers in church before Mr. and Mrs. Watson died and before their young-uns—all but Yodel—scattered here and yon. 'Lord, please don't let the Watsons sit near us.' And, 'Lord, please stop up my ears just long enough to deliver me from sufferin' through another hymn.' And, 'Lord, please give Tar laryngitis for forty-five minutes.'"

We both laughed.

"That was ugly of me to tell," Myra said. "But it's true! Still, I'll have to ask forgiveness for that. I always did wonder if God hadn't blessed any of them Watsons with musical ability because they'd tried to write their own ticket with those musical names. You know what I mean?"

"I guess you've got a point there."

"Anyhow, back to Yodel. Yodel was jealous of China York because China could sing. The choir director was always getting China to sing solos. China didn't care for Yodel because Yodel was spiteful and mean to her most of the time. It seemed Yodel couldn't feel good about herself unless she was puttin' somebody else down."

"She must've felt great about herself every time I brought a cake over," I muttered. "Sorry. Go on."

"Well, a few years ago, our old preacher retired and we got a new one. Of course, we threw him a potluck howdy-get-to-know-you party at the church. It was summer, and I took a strawberry pie. I make the best strawberry pies. I'd thought about making one for Thanksgiving, but I don't have to now that you've given me all these cakes. I do appreciate it."

I waved away her gratitude. "Don't mention it."

"Anyhow, China brought a chocolate and coconut cake. She'd got the recipe out of *McCall's* magazine and was just bustin' to have us all try out this cake. Wouldn't you know it?

In waltzed Yodel with the very same cake."

"If she loved to bake so much, I wonder why she gave it up. She told me she didn't have time to bake these days. Was she active in a lot of groups? I mean, what took up so much of her time?"

"Keeping tabs on the rest of the town took up her time. When Arlo was alive—he was a Watson, too, of course, though no relation . . . except maybe really distant cousins once or twice removed or something . . . There's more Watsons in these parts than there are chins . . . at a fat farm. Is that how that saying goes?"

"I think it's more Chins than a Chinese phone book."

"Huh. I don't get it. Anyhow, Arlo expected his wife to be more than the town gossip. That's when Yodel prided herself on her cooking, her volunteer work and all the rest. When he died—oh, I guess it was ten years ago—she gave all that up." She shook her head. "Shame, too. But, back to the story. Yodel told the new preacher, 'Wait until you try this cake. It's my very own recipe.'

"'It is not,' China said. 'You saw me copy that recipe out of *McCall's* when we were both at the beauty shop waitin' to get our hair done!'

"'So what if I did?' Yodel asked.

"'You had to have heard me tell Mary that I was making this cake for the potluck.'

"Oooh, China was boiling. But Yodel just shrugged and said, 'I subscribe to *McCall's*. How was I supposed to know you'd be making a similar cake?'

"China got right up in Yodel's face and hollered, 'It's the same cake!'

"Yodel said it wasn't. She said, 'I put almonds and a splash of vanilla in mine. Otherwise that cake would be boring and bland.'

"At this point, the preacher tried to intervene. 'They both look delicious,' he told them, 'and I'm sure there are enough of us here to eat them both.'

"Yodel's and China's eyes were locked like two snarling

dogs, and I don't believe either of them heard a word he said. China had already set her cake on the table, but Yodel was still holding hers. China calmly placed her hand on the bottom of Yodel's cake plate and upended that cake right on Yodel's chest."

I giggled. "Really?"

"Really. And then China walked to the door and said, 'I've had it with her. I won't be back here until one of us is dead.' And she ain't been back to church since."

"Wow," I said. "That's some story."

"Makes you wonder if China finally got tired of sitting home by herself on Sunday mornings."

Seeing how serious Myra looked, I stifled my laughter. "Do you honestly think this woman has been nursing a grudge all these years and killed Mrs. Watson rather than simply finding herself another church?"

"There's not another Baptist church within ten miles of here." She finished off her soda. "People have killed for crazier reasons than that, haven't they?"

"I suppose, but—"

"And if it wasn't China York, I can think of a few other folks who had it in for Yodel."

"Come on. I'll admit she's been a pain to work with on these cakes, but I have a hard time casting Mrs. Watson in the role of Cruella De Vil."

Myra got up and put her empty soda can in the garbage. "I didn't say she made puppy coats. I said there were a lot of people who'd just as soon not have Yodel Watson around."

Coming in 2010
Daphne's Next Cake-Baking Mystery
KILLER SWEET TOOTH

## Book Three in the Daphne Martin Cake Decorating Mystery Series

It all began with a little bite of innocent sweetness. It was mid-January, and Brea Ridge had been experiencing the type of "Desperado" days the Eagles would describe as "the sky won't snow and the sun won't shine." Indeed, it was hard to tell the nighttime from the day.

Ben, my significant other—at least, to my way of thinking . . . and I believe he's thinking that way, too, after the comment he made just before Christmas—was working late on a story. He's a reporter, editor and go-to-guy for the *Brea Ridge Chronicle*. On top of that, he's a perfectionist who has trouble delegating. Hence, the working late.

Violet, my sister, was visiting her mother-in-law this evening with her hubby Jason and my precious tween twin nephew and niece Lucas and Leslie. Try saying that line three times fast. Anyway, Grammy Armstrong was celebrating her seventieth birthday, and Violet's family as well as the rest of the Armstrong clan was gathering to wish her well.

All of which, I must selfishly admit, left me out in the cold. Pardon the pun. But I was lonely. Lucky for me—or, at least, I thought so at the time—Myra was lonely, too. Myra is my favorite neighbor. She's a sassy, sixty-something (you'll never get her to admit to any specific age) widow who knows everything about everybody in Brea Ridge (or can find out), who has a heart of gold and who is as entertaining as they come. I gave her a call and she agreed to come over for some just-made cashew brittle and a game of Scrabble. Myra tends to make up words when playing Scrabble, but that merely adds to the challenge of the game.

At the sound of the doorbell, Sparrow, my one-eyed formerly-stray gray and white Persian cat raced down the hall toward my office. She has a little bed in there under the desk, and it's her favorite hiding place. She has begrudgingly made friends with me, but she isn't comfortable around other people yet. Don't worry about the one-eye. The veterinarian said she was probably born that way. Plus, it's how she got her name. Lucas and Leslie named her Sparrow in honor of Captain Jack, Johnny Depp's character in *Pirates of the Caribbean*. They said having one eye made Sparrow look like a pirate.

I opened the door and Myra came in wearing jeans, an oversized blue sweater and a pair of Ugg boots. She deposited the boots by the door and rubbed her hands together.

"I'm so glad you called," she said. "I've been bored out of my mind today."

"Me, too," I said. "Cake orders have been slow since New Year's."

"They'll pick back up."

We walked into the kitchen where I had the Scrabble board set up on the island. The two stools were set on opposite sides of the island. The cashew brittle, popcorn and chocolate-covered raisins were plated and on a tray to the right side of the board. The Scrabble tiles were to the left.

"What would you like to drink?" I asked.

"Something hot. How about a decaf café au lait?"

I smiled. "Sounds good to me."

Myra sat down and began choosing her tiles. "Great. Nearly all vowels. How am I supposed to make a word out of this mess?"

"Just put those back and draw some new letters." I have a single-cup coffee maker, so I began making Myra's café au lait.

"No, now, you know I don't cheat," she said. "I'll make do with the letters I have. Maybe some of this cashew brittle will help me think."

The next sound I heard was a howl of pain.

"Myra? What is it?"

"Owwww, my toof . . . my filling . . . fell out!" She rocked back and forth on the stool.

I turned the coffee maker off. "Who's your dentist? I'll call him and ask if he can meet you in his office." Don't think I was being sexist when I said "him." There are only two dentists in Brea Ridge, and they're both men.

"Bainworf."

I got "Bainsworth" out of the mumbled word and rushed into the living room to retrieve my phone book from the end table. I called the dentist's office and then dialed the emergency number left on the answering machine. Dr. Bainsworth answered the call immediately.

"Hi, Dr. Bainsworth. I'm Daphne Martin. A patient of yours—Myra Jenkins—is here at my house. She bit into a piece of cashew brittle and lost a filling. She's in terrible pain."

"Ah, yes, I know Myra well. Tell her I'll meet her at my office in a half hour. In the meantime, do you have any clove oil?"

"I believe so."

"Then apply a little of the oil to the tooth with a cotton swab," he said. "It'll help dull the pain until you can get her here." He chuckled. "Good luck."

"Thank you." Apparently, he *did* know Myra well.

I returned to the kitchen. "Dr. Bainsworth will see you in his office in half an hour."

"Half an hour? I'll be dead by then."

I opened the cabinet where I keep my spices and got the clove oil. "He told me to apply a little of this to your tooth with a cotton swab. He said it will help dull the pain."

"Easy for him to say." She continued moaning as I went to the bathroom for a cotton swab.

"Come on," I said, when I had both clove oil and cotton swab in hand. "Dr. Bainsworth says this will help. Take your hand down, open your mouth and show me which tooth."

She opened her mouth. "It's 'is toot." She pointed to her second bicuspid on the left. "The one throbbing wit pain."

I dabbed clove oil on the tooth. "There. Feel better?"

"No."

"Well, just give it a minute. Go ahead and get your boots back on, and we'll go on to the dentist's office."

She got down from the stool, went into the living room and got on her boots. It was a laborious effort, but she managed somehow.

I took my coat from the closet, grabbed my purse and car keys and off we went.

Myra gasped and covered her mouth when the cold air hit her tooth.

"I'm sorry," I told her, "but the dentist is meeting us, and you'll be feeling better in no time."

She nodded as I opened the passenger side door of my red Mini Cooper and helped her get in.

I hurried around to the driver's side, started the engine, turned on the lights and backed out of the driveway. The traffic was surprisingly heavy for a mid-week winter's night in Brea Ridge. We met at least half a dozen cars on the way to Dr. Bainsworth's office.

When we got there, I was relieved to see lights blazing in the back of the office. Dr. Bainsworth was already here and, presumably, had everything ready to fix Myra's tooth.

Myra pulled the neck of her sweater up over the lower portion of her face before stepping out into the cold air. I walked ahead of her so I could hold the heavy door open for her.

We stepped inside and looked around the empty office. Empty offices always look creepy at night, don't you think? There was only one light on in the entryway; and in the waiting area, the long, skinny windows allowed muted light from streetlamps to filter in casting shadows throughout the room.

"Dr. Bainsworth? It's Daphne Martin and Myra Jenkins. Would you like us to come on back?"

He didn't answer, and I supposed maybe he couldn't hear us.

"Let's go on back," I said to Myra.

She nodded slightly, and we walked back toward the

examining rooms.

"Dr. Bainsworth?" I called again. "Are you back here?"

I looked inside the first exam room. My eyes widened, and my hand flew to my throat. I turned to Myra in shocked silence.

"Wha?" She followed my gaze to where Dr. Bainsworth was lying facedown on the floor. A trickle of blood emanated from his head. "No!"

"It's okay," I said, putting my arms around her. "I'll call 9-1-1. I'm sure he'll be all right."

"My toof! Who'll fix my toof!"

I heard a noise in the front office and froze. Myra did, too.

"Whoever did this to Dr. Bainsworth is still here," I whispered.

She nodded.

"We have to find weapons." I stepped into the examining room and grabbed a huge plastic toothbrush.

Myra armed herself with a model of a molar so big she could barely hold it. She raised it up to eye level so she'd be ready to strike someone with it if need be.

It was at that moment that we heard the sirens. Which was odd because I hadn't called 9-1-1 yet.

I looked from my giant toothbrush to Myra's giant molar to the dentist bleeding on the floor. "This is not good."

More Great Cozy Mysteries From Bell Bridge Books

Dixie Divas
Book One, The Dixie Divas Series
Virginia Brown
Now Available!
Trade Paperback
Ebook at Fictionwise.com


Excerpt

## CHAPTER 1

If not for long-dead Civil War Generals Ulysses S. Grant, Nathan Bedford Forrest, and a pot of chicken and dumplings, Bitty Hollandale would never have been charged with murder. Of course, if the mule hadn't eaten the chicken and dumplings, that would have helped a lot, too.

My name is Eureka Truevine, but my family and friends all call me Trinket. Except for my ex-husband, who's been known to call me a few other names. That's one of the reasons I left him and came home to take care of my parents who are in their second adolescence, having missed out on their first one for reasons of survival.

We live at Cherryhill in Mississippi, three miles outside of Holly Springs and forty-five minutes down 78 Highway southeast from Memphis, Tennessee. My father— Edward Wellford Truevine— inherited the house from my grandparents around fifty years ago. It wasn't in great shape when he got it, but over the years he's put money, time, and his own craftsmanship into it, and now it's on the Holly Springs Historic Register.

Every April, Holly Springs has an annual pilgrimage tour of restored antebellum homes, with pretty girls and women in hoop skirts and high button shoes. Men and boys in

Confederate uniforms stand sentry with old family Sharpshooters and cavalry swords, neither of which could do much harm to a marshmallow. It's a big event that draws people from all over the country and gives purpose to the lives of more than a few elderly matrons and historical buffs.

This year, Bitty Hollandale cooked up a big pot of chicken and dumplings to take to Mr. Sanders, who lives in an old house off Highway 7 that the local historical society has been trying to get on the historic register for decades. Sherman Sanders is known for his fondness of chicken and dumplings, and Bitty meant to convince him to put his house on the tour. It'd been built in 1832 and kept in remarkably good shape. Most of the original furniture is in most of the original places, with most of the original wallpaper and carpets still in their original places. The only modern renovations have been electricity and what's discreetly referred to as a water closet. It's enough to make any Southerner drool with envy and avarice.

"Go with me, Trinket," Bitty said to me that day in February. "It'd be such a feather in my cap to get the Sanders house on our tour."

I looked over at my parents. My father was dressed in plaid golfing pants and a red striped shirt, and my mother wore a red cable knit sweater and a plaid skirt. Under the kitchen table at their feet lay their little brown dog, appropriately named Little Brown Dog and called Brownie. He wore a red plaid sweater. They all like to coordinate.

"I don't know," I said doubtfully to Bitty. "I'm not sure what our plans are for the day."

What I really meant was I wasn't at all sure leaving my parents alone would be wise. Since I've come home, I've noticed they have a tendency to pretend they're sixteen again. While their libidos may be, their bodies are still mid-seventies. The doctor assures me it's fine, but I worry about them. Daddy's had an angioplasty, and Mama has occasional lapses of memory. But otherwise, they're probably in better shape than Bitty and me.

Bitty, like me, is fifty-one, a little on the plump side, and divorced. But she's lived in Holly Springs all her life, while I haven't come back to live since I married and followed my husband to random jobs around the country. Bitty and I have been close since we were six years old and she rode over on her pony to invite me to a swimming party. As I then had a love for anything to do with horses, she fast became my best friend. Besides that, she's my first cousin. I've got other cousins in the area, but over the years we've lost touch and haven't gotten around to getting reacquainted.

Bitty knows everyone. I've only been back a couple of months and am still struggling to reacquaint myself with old friends. Some people I remember from my childhood, but many have been forgotten over the years. Besides, the shock of finding my parents so different from how I remembered them in my childhood still hasn't faded enough to encourage more shocks of the same kind.

"They'll be just fine," Bitty assured me. She knew what made me hesitate. "Uncle Eddie and Aunt Anna can do without you for an hour."

"Maybe you're right." I studied Mama and Daddy. They played gin rummy with a pack of cards that looked as if they'd survived the Blitzkrieg. "Will you two be okay if I run an errand with Bitty?" I asked in a loud enough voice to catch their attention.

"Gin!" my mother shouted triumphantly, or what passes for a shout with her. She's petite, with flawless ivory skin that's never seen a blemish or freckle, bright blue eyes, and stylishly short silver hair that used to be blond. Next to my father, who's over six-four in his stockinged feet, she looks like a child's doll. My father has brown eyes and the kind of skin that looks like he works in the sun. He wears a neatly trimmed mustache, his once dark brown hair is still thick, but has been white since a family tragedy in the late sixties. He reminds me of an older Rhett Butler. Since I'm using *Gone With the Wind* references, my mother reminds me of Melanie Wilkes, with just enough Scarlett O'Hara thrown in to keep her interesting. And unpredictable.

I, on the other hand, am more like Scarlett's sister Suellen, with just enough of Mammy's pragmatic optimism to keep me from being a complete cynic and whiner. I inherited my father's height, my grandmother's tendency toward weight gain, and auburn hair and green eyes no one can explain. I like to think I'm a throwback to my mother's Scotch-Irish ancestry.

"We'll be fine if your mother will stop cheating at cards," my father said.

Mama just smiled. "I'm not cheating, Eddie. I'm just good enough to win."

Daddy shook his head. "You've got to be cheating. No one beats me at gin."

"Except me."

"So," I said again, a little louder, "you'll both be fine for a little while, right?"

My mother looked at me with surprise. "Of course, sugar," she said. "We're always fine."

Bitty and I went out to her car. Bitty's real name is Elisabeth, but it got shortened to Bitty when she was born and the name stuck. Anyone who calls her Elisabeth is a stranger or works for the government. Bitty is one of those females who attract men like state taxpayers' money lures politicians. On her, a little extra weight settles in the form of voluptuous curves. About five-two in her Prada pumps, she has blond hair, china blue eyes, a complexion like a California girl, and a laugh that'd make even Scrooge smile. If she wasn't my best friend, I'd probably be jealous.

"I wish you'd drive a bigger car," I complained once I'd wedged myself into her flashy red sports car that smelled of chicken and dumplings. "I always feel like a giant in this thing."

Bitty shifted the car into gear and we lurched forward. "You are a giant."

"I am not. I'm statuesque. Five-nine is not that tall for a woman. Though I admit I could lose twenty pounds and not miss it."

Gears ground and I winced as we pulled out of the driveway onto the road that leads to Highway 311. One of the things Bitty got in her last— and fourth— divorce was a lot of money that she's found new and interesting ways to spend. I got ulcers from my one and only divorce. Those aren't bankable. My only child, however, a married daughter, makes up for everything.

It was one of those February days that promise good weather isn't so far away. Yellow daffodils and tufts of crocus bloomed in yards and outlined empty spaces where houses had once been. Some fields had already been plowed in preparation for spring planting. A few puffy clouds skimmed across a bright blue sky, and sunlight through the Miata's windshield heated the car. I rolled down my window and inhaled essence of Mississippi. It was cool, familiar, and very nice.

"So what are you going to do with yourself, Trinket?"

I looked over at Bitty. "What do you mean?"

"You've been home almost three months now. A doctor just bought Easthaven. Want me to introduce you?"

"Good Lord, no. I don't want another man in my life."

"He's a podiatrist. Think of how useful that could be. And Easthaven is one of the nicest houses in Holly Springs."

"My feet are fine. And Cherryhill suits me right now." Bitty ground another gear and I checked my seatbelt. Undaunted by my lack of interest, she went right on talking.

"Think of the future. Once your parents are gone, God forbid, you'll be all alone in that big ole rambling house. Is that what you want?"

"Dear Lord, yes. Not that I want my parents gone, but living alone doesn't bother me. I'm used to it. Perry traveled a lot."

"Whatever possessed you to marry a man named Percival, anyway? It sounds like a name out of Chaucer's medieval romances."

"His mother read a lot. Besides, with a name like Eureka Truevine, that's not a stone I felt I should throw."

Bitty nodded. "That's true enough. Percival and Eureka Berryman. Good thing his last name isn't Berry. Then he'd be Perry Berry."

We laughed. It's funny what appeals to middle-aged women past their prime but not their youthfulness. There's a sense of freedom in being beyond some expectations.

When we pulled up into the rutted driveway of The Cedars where Sherman Sanders lives in voluntary isolation and bachelorhood, he was sitting on his colonnaded front porch, serenely rocking with a shotgun across his lap. He stood up, a small man with wizened features, bowed legs, and a nose that juts out like a ship's prow. He wore faded blue overalls, muddy boots that had long ago lost any kind of shape, a flannel shirt that had seen better days, and a straw hat that looked like something big had taken a bite out of one side. A bone-thin black and tan hound lay beside the rocking chair, and when Sanders nudged it with his boot, the old dog struggled to its feet and bayed in the opposite direction. Sherman Sanders casually brought up the shotgun. It pointed straight at Bitty's car. He obviously had better eyesight than his hound.

"Don't mind the shotgun," Bitty said when I made a squeaking sound. "He doesn't shoot women. Usually."

"Dear Lord," I got out in that squeaky tone. "Who does he usually shoot?"

Bitty opened her car door and stuck her head out. She waved her hand and called, "Yoo hoo, Mr. Sanders, it's Bitty Hollandale. You remember me?"

Sanders aimed a stream of brown spit at the dirt in front of the house and nodded. "Yep. I 'member you. You're that pesky female that's been worryin' the hell out of me 'bout my house."

One thing about Bitty, she never lets minor obstacles deter her from her goal.

She smiled real big. "That's right. I brought you something."

Sanders shifted the wad of tobacco in his mouth to his other cheek. "Don't need nuthin'. Might as well go on back home. I ain't in'trested in my house bein' on no stupid damn tour with a bunch of strangers walkin' through it and gawkin' at everything."

I didn't much blame him, but I didn't say that to Bitty.

"Oh, you'll like this," she said, and started to put both feet out of the car to reach in the back for the pot of chicken and dumplings. Unfortunately, she'd forgotten to take the car out of gear or set the brake. The Miata bucked forward. Off-guard, Bitty pitched out of the car like a sack of cornmeal and sprawled face-first onto red dirt. Luckily, she was wearing a pantsuit and not a skirt, but her rear end stuck up in the air like a generous red wool flag. The car coughed, died, and made an annoying buzzing sound.

Sherman Sanders cackled so loud his hound started to bark again, turning its head in all different directions just in case the mysterious noise was dangerous. While Mr. Sanders slapped his thigh and cackled, I set the brake, took the keys out of the ignition to stop the buzzing, then got out and went over to see if Bitty was hurt.

"Are you okay?" I asked anxiously, but could tell she was just more mad than anything else. She sat up and brushed dirt and gravel from her face, palms, and the front of her pants.

"Damn car. I keep forgetting it's got a clutch. Look at my pants. I just got them out of the cleaners, too. Give me a hand up, will you?"

I did and she turned back to Mr. Sanders. "As I was saying, you'll like this, Mr. Sanders. It's your favorite."

Bitty has always been quite resilient.

"Oh my, where _are_ my manners?" she said then, and gave me a push forward. "Mr. Sanders, this is my cousin, Trinket Truevine from over at Cherryhill."

I managed a polite smile and "How do you do" while keeping an eye on the shotgun, but a still chortling Sanders looked like what I often call, "ain't right," meaning not right in the head.

Bitty pulled out the big aluminum pot where she'd secured it behind the driver's seat, and marched relentlessly up to the porch. When she set it down on the white-painted hickory planks, the hound immediately found it irresistible. Its nose seemed to be the only one of the five senses still working efficiently.

"Sit, Tuck," Mr. Sanders said, again with another nudge, and the dog reluctantly squatted on its back haunches with nose in the air and sniffing furiously. Sanders leaned forward. "What you got in that pot?"

Bitty smiled. "Chicken and dumplings. Homemade, of course."

I could see Sanders wavering. The shotgun lowered, the bowed legs quivered, and I swear that his nose twitched just like his hound's.

"Huh. Reckon you intend to bribe me with those, do you."

"I sure do." Bitty's smile got bigger. She lifted the lid and a thin curl of steam wafted up. "Fresh, too. Just made early this morning. They have to sit a little bit to let the dumplings soak up all that broth, of course."

"Young hen?"

"Two. And White Lily flour cut with shortening and rolled out to a quarter inch."

While they discussed the intricacies of dumplings, I looked around. The white painted house has a chimney at each end; old brick covered with ivy at one end, bare wisteria limbs on the other chimney. Windows go all the way to porch level on the front, with green shutters that can be closed in stormy or cold weather. Elongated *S* hooks have the patina of age on them, but still look in good working order. A lantern hangs from the center of the porch, and electrical wire covered with conduit pipes painted white run along the porch's edge to make a sharp right angle beside the double front door, and then run parallel above the footings of the house and around the corner. One of the front doors was open, the screen shut. The closed door has one of those old-fashioned bells that have to be twisted to make a noise. It's a bright, polished brass. Everything about the house promises loving attention, while the front yard looks like goats live in it. No grass. Just red dirt, ruts, and gigantic cedar trees with furrowed gray trunks splintery with age.

"Reckon you can come in if you want," I heard Sanders say, and I looked over at Bitty. I thought she might faint. Her face had the dazed expression of someone in a spiritual trance.

Her voice shook a little when she said faintly, "Why, Mr. Sanders, we'd love to come in. Wouldn't we, Trinket?"

I looked at the shotgun. I wasn't so sure.

"Uh..."

"Come on, Tuck," Sanders said, and opened the screen door for us. "He don't bite, but I ain't of a mind to leave him out here with that pot."

The hound didn't worry me. When it'd drooled over the chicken and dumplings, I'd seen that it had no front teeth. Mr. Sanders, however, seemed to have all of his teeth but not all of his marbles. Maybe it was the odd glint in his eyes, or the way he kept cackling like an old hen.

Reluctantly, I followed Bitty and Sanders into the house. It has that smell old houses have of meals long eaten, people long past, memories long gone. It isn't a bad smell. It's actually very comforting. Furniture gleamed dully, smelling like lemony beeswax. Bitty paused in the entrance hall and took in a deep breath. She was obviously having a religious experience.

As if afraid to wake the saints of old houses, she whispered, "Beautiful. Just beautiful!"

I have to admit she's right. Oval-framed photographs of family members in garments a hundred and forty years old hang on walls. The walnut mantel over the fireplace holds more old photos in small frames, a chunky bronze statue of a soldier on a horse, and a pair of crystal candlesticks. A low fire burned behind solid brass andirons. The front room is filled with antiques, and just a glimpse into the dining room across the foyer promised more treasures in the heavy furniture and wide sideboards against two walls.

Since I don't know that much about antiques or old houses, I followed along as Mr. Sanders gave us the royal tour. Bitty kept clasping her hands in front of her face as if praying, and murmured in rapture while we looked at huge old beds with wooden canopies and mosquito netting, cedar wardrobes that go all the way to the ceiling and still hold clothes from the 1800s, and gilded mirrors with a mottled tinge betraying their age. Carpets laid over bare heart-pine floors look as if they hadn't been walked on in years.

By the time the tour was over, Bitty had almost convinced Sanders to allow his house to be put on the historic register and added to the tour. He still had reservations and muttered about turning his home into a circus, but had definitely wavered. *Bitty really is good. She should sell real estate or run for Congress.*

When we got down to the foyer again with Tuck tagging along at our heels, Bitty picked up a bronze statue from a small parquet table. "This is General Grant, isn't it?" she asked.

For the historically uninformed, General Grant was a Civil War general who burned and slashed his way across Mississippi in 1862, but spared most of Holly Springs. Legend says it was because the ladies were so pretty and treated him to nightly piano concerts, but historical fact has a different version.

Ulysses Sherman Sanders was named in honor of Generals Grant and Sherman, since his family had taken possession of The Cedars right after the war when taxes were high and Confederate income non-existent. As Yankees, they were not enthusiastically welcomed into the community. A few generations have gone by since then and hostilities have ceased for the most part, even if not been completely forgotten by some.

Sanders bristled at any hint of censure in Bitty's question. "That's right; it's a statue of General Grant. Got a problem with that?"

"Heavens no. General Grant was an absolute gentleman while he and his troops stayed in Holly Springs, though I can't say the same for all his soldiers. With some exceptions, of course," she added hastily, apparently remembering that Sherman Sanders' ancestor had been one of those Union soldiers. "This statue's very heavy. Is it weighted?"

Sanders nodded. "I reckon so. Probably because it'd be top heavy otherwise, what with the general liftin' his sword like that."

Bitty smiled and set it down carefully. "I'll be back in a day or two to discuss what needs to be done before the tour. Even though The Cedars hasn't yet been put on the historic register, we can fill out the paperwork and submit it. I don't think there'll be any problem at all. You've done such a wonderful job taking care of this house. I honestly don't think there's another house in Marshall County that's been kept up nearly this well. Most need extensive renovations."

Sanders puffed up his chest. He still held his shotgun, but just by the barrel now. I hoped that was a good sign.

Tuck suddenly barked and rushed toward the open screen door, making me jump. We all looked outside. Something big and brown had its head stuck in the pot of chicken and dumplings. Before Bitty or I could move, Sanders started to cussing, and banged out the screen door and took a shot at the aluminum pot. Rock salt pellets pinged against metal, and the mule made a strangled sound and took off down the rutted drive wearing the pot up to its eyeballs and shedding chicken and dumplings behind it. Tuck immediately took advantage of this unexpected windfall, and the pot-blinded mule ran into a tree. The impact knocked it backwards so that it sat on its haunches blinking dumplings from its eyes while the liberated pot rolled across the yard. Tuck greedily and happily worked the path the pot had taken, slurping loudly. The mule got up and shook itself free of dumplings, obviously unharmed. And unfazed.

Bitty and I just stood there transfixed by the entire thing. Mr. Sanders heaved a disgusted sigh.

"Blamed mule," he said. "I swear it's part goat. Ate half my hat last week."

Roused from temporary astonishment, Bitty said brightly, "Well, I'll just have to cook you up another big batch of chicken and dumplings. Don't worry about the pot. I have another one at home."

We were halfway back to Cherryhill before we started laughing. Bitty had to pull over to the side of the road so we wouldn't wreck. Finally I wiped tears from my eyes and tried to keep from snorting through my nose. I have a tendency to do that when I'm hysterical with laughter.

"Is putting this house on the tour worth another pot of chicken and dumplings?" I asked as soon as I was snort-free.

Bitty nodded. "As many as it takes. I'll just have to buy more ingredients and take them over to Sharita's house."

"You fraud. Someone else cooked them for you?"

"Good Lord, Trinket, you know I can't cook. If I'd cooked them we'd have been shot, stuffed, and mounted over that magnificent walnut mantel. Did you see it? All those gorgeous hunting scenes carved into the wood... I thought I'd pass out from pure pleasure."

Bitty and I have different values in many ways. While I appreciate antiques and old houses and generations of custom, it's more in an abstract kind of way. Bitty has obviously made it her reason for living. There are different ways of handling divorce and that empty feeling you get even if the relationship degenerated into nastiness and you're happy to see the last of him. My divorce was pretty straightforward. Bitty's last divorce made waves throughout the entire state.

Bitty let me off in front of my house. "I'm going shopping for new shoes," she said, and tooled on down our circular drive with a happy wave of her hand. I smiled and shook my head. Now there's a woman who knows how to cope.

Mama and Daddy had gone from playing gin to planning a cruise. Pamphlets were spread over the kitchen table. Something familiar smelling simmered on the stove, and afternoon light made cozy patterns on the walls and floor. Brownie slept in a patch of sunshine. He's a beagle-dachshund mix with long legs, a short body, a dachshund head and coloring, and a beagle's loud bay. He can be heard three counties over when he scents a squirrel. He's also neurotic.

"Where are you going?" I asked my parents when I'd hung my sweater on a coat hook beside the back door and stood looking over Daddy's shoulder at the array of pamphlets.

"I was thinking we'd enjoy rafting down the Colorado

River. But your mother wants to take the Delta Queen down to New Orleans. They have a cruise in March this year. It's usually June before the cruises start, but it's been chartered just for us retired postal employees."

Mama looked up. "I thought it'd be nice to travel down the river like those old gamblers used to do. Do you remember _Maverick_? Not the movie. The old TV show. James Garner always did well. I have a feeling I might be just as lucky."

"Huh," Daddy said. "You just think you're a card shark now because you beat me at gin."

"Three times," Mama said with a big smile.

I thought it best not to interfere. "What's for supper?" I asked instead.

"Chicken and dumplings."

My parents just looked at me as if I'd lost my mind when I started laughing, and I heard Mama say to Daddy in a low tone, "Hormones. Must be The Change."

Cart Before The Corpse
Book One
The Merry Abbott Carriage Driving Mysteries
Set in Mossy Creek
Carolyn McSparren
Trade Paperback 14.95
Ebook at Fictionwise.com


Excerpt


Chapter 1
*Sunday Afternoon, Chattanooga, Tennessee*


*Merry*


I should learn to count chickens instead of eggs.

I'd already packed my computer and printer in my truck and checked out of my motel. The scores were posted on all the driving classes except the cross- country marathon. As show manager, I'd passed out ribbons and trophies. Once the marathon ended and the scores were tallied, I could drive away from the horseshow grounds with a happy grin and a fat check.

That's when I heard the screams. "Runaway!" I turned and raced across the field toward the start of the marathon course. When the screams continued, I knew this was more than a loose trace.

Please God some nervous horse had yanked his lead line from his groom and wandered off to graze, or decided he didn't feel like being harnessed to his carriage today and trotted away dragging his reins and harness behind him.

Just so long as he wasn't also dragging a carriage.

A runaway horse harnessed to a driverless carriage is a four-legged missile with no guidance system.

I was still fifty yards from the start of the marathon course when I saw Jethro, Pete and Tully Hull's Morgan stallion kick out with both hind feet and connect with the steel dashboard of their heavy marathon cart with a God-awful clang. Terrified, Jethro reared straight up in his traces and tossed both Pete and Tully off the carriage and into the dirt.

"He's going over backwards!" somebody screamed.

Amy Hull, Pete and Tully's thirteen-year-old daughter, clung to the back of the carriage. Her normal job was as counterbalance around fast turns. Now, she was trying to keep both Jethro and the carriage from landing on top of her.

"Jump and roll, Amy!" I shouted. "Get out of the way!"

She jumped, landed on her feet and rolled away from the carriage. With less weight to overbalance him, Jethro came down solidly on all fours, Thank God.

But then he took off at a dead run across the field, with the carriage careening wildly after him.

Still screaming warnings, some people ran to help the Hulls. Competitors stamped on their carriage brakes and reined their own horses in hard to keep the course from erupting into a re-run of the chariot race in *Ben Hur*. Poor Jethro was terrified. With the eighteen-foot reins flying behind him, the carriage had become his personal banshee. He had to escape it if it killed him.

It might. As well some of the rest of us, horses, competitors, trainers and spectators alike, if we didn't stop him. And nobody else was trying. Everybody not rushing to help the Hulls dove out of the way, cowered behind trucks and horse vans, huddled in the tents with the food and the vendors and prayed that Jethro wouldn't decide to charge them.

Jethro weighed three quarters of a ton. The steel marathon carriage weighed only slightly less. The horse had become a runaway eighteen-wheeler with four legs and a terrified brain.

He craved sanctuary. He was desperate to find his people so they could get the monster off his tail. He didn't know he'd left them behind in the dirt. Somehow I had to focus his attention on *me*, let him know that one human being wanted to save him from the monster that chased him.

He swerved past a four-wheeled spider phaeton pulled by

a huge black Friesian gelding. Friesians were originally bred to carry Lancelot in full knightly armor, so they're graceful but massive. The axels passed one another with barely room for a single piece of blotting paper between them. Anne Crawford, on the Friesian's reins, stood up and screamed. Her Queen Mary hat with its pheasant tail and orange tulle flew off her head and landed on the Friesian's broad rump. The Friesian kicked at it.

The hat fell in the dirt and the Friesian relaxed, thank the Lord.

Jethro spun through a ninety-degree corner around the stables. The carriage rocked dangerously but righted itself. Then he headed straight for the parking area where over forty trailers and trucks were closely aligned in rows.

I ran to cut Jethro off, waved my arms and yelled to get his attention in hopes he'd be so startled he'd pull up or swerve away before he reached the narrow lanes between the vehicles.

He knew how wide *his* body was, and that he could fit between the trailers and trucks. He didn't have a clue how wide the carriage behind him was. If it stuck hard, he'd be yanked up on a dime. The steel carriage might disintegrate.

Jethro could break his neck. Carriages are replaceable. Jethro was not.

Jethro galloped straight at me. Behind him the carriage caromed from side to side and clanged as it side-swiped trailers and trucks like the steel ball in a pinball machine.

At the last minute, I dove between a silver *dually* and a bright red Ford Two-Fifty truck as Jethro thundered by, still pursued by his invisible banshee. If he even noticed me, he darned well didn't care. I wasn't one of *his* people. He headed for the access road, the only paved road on the farm the road that cars and trucks drove on--cars and trucks that might collide head-on with Jethro.

I sprinted across the field in front of the stable. If I could get ahead of him . . . He came out from between the final pair of horse trailers and swerved onto the road as I reached it.

Without warning, his aluminum shoes slipped on the

paving, and all four feet flew out from under him. He crashed onto his side and tipped the carriage. His sharp hooves flailed the air.

I knew he'd start struggling to his feet in about ten seconds. I did the only thing I could do. I yanked off my jacket, tossed it over his head, sat on his neck and leaned both hands on his shoulder.

The minute I covered his eyes and he felt my weight, Jethro relaxed. He was drenched with sweat, his sides heaved, and every muscle trembled, but in his mind the banshee wasn't after him any longer, although I could still hear the wheels spinning behind him. I didn't dare turn to look.

"Somebody undo the girth! Unhook the tugs and the traces!" I shouted over my shoulder. "Get this carriage off him!" He shivered and struggled, but quieted when I spoke to him gently and caressed his sweaty neck.

"You're okay, sweetie," I whispered. I could recite nursery rhymes so long as my voice stayed calm and my hands caressed his neck. He trusted that I could free him of the banshee. Behind me, I heard people shouting, calling for knives to cut the harness free. Careful to keep his eyes covered, I rocked Jethro up on his shoulder just far enough to allow the steel shaft under him to be pulled free, then pressed his headdown once more onto the pavement. A minute later, both shafts slid backward away from the horse. I couldn't take my eyes off him, but I could hear people grunting as they shifted the weight of the carriage. I kept stroking and talking.

After what seemed like an eternity I felt a hand on my shoulder. "Merry, we've got the carriage up and the harness free. Time to get him up." My heart lurched. So long as Jethro stayed quiet under me, so long as he didn't scramble to his feet and try to walk, we didn't have to assess his injuries.

I didn't want to know. If he'd broken a leg . . .

The first thing you learn around horses is how fragile they are in mind and body. You protect them and care for them as well as you can. Sometimes that's not enough, but it's the job we sign on for. They can't take care of themselves I'd tried to help Jethro, but I had no idea whether I'd been successful.

"Merry, I'm going to haul you back away from him on your butt. Don't want you catching a hoof in the head when he tries to stand." I felt strong hands under my armpits. I knew the voice. Jack, the Johnsons' groom. Probably strong enough to lift *Jethro* if he had to. He swung me away and to my feet as though I weighed about as much as a little Jack Russell Terrier, then dropped a heavy brown arm across my shoulders and turned me against his chest. Behind me I heard Jethro's hooves scrabbling. "He's up, Merry. You can look."

I felt Jethro's warm breath against my neck as I faced him and leaned my shoulder against his. "Please be okay," I whispered. Jack hooked a hand on his bridle, but Jethro was too worn out to go anywhere. The stallion took a tentative step, snorted once to frighten any residue of banshee away, then took two more steps. He walked 'dead sound,' meaning without injury, in civilian terms. He was bleeding from a couple of shallow cuts on his shoulder, probably from collisions with the fenders of trailers. He'd scraped himself a bit from the asphalt on the road, but the damage was minor. A few stitches, a little Betadine antiseptic, and he'd be fine. Amazing that he hadn't ripped a leg tendon on the fender of a truck or gashed himself to the bone on a trailer door.

"Merry, honey," Jack said, "Idn't that your good leather jacket?"

I looked down. It was the only thing I'd had to toss over Jethro's head. He now stood with his front hooves squarely in the middle of four hundred bucks worth of tan suede.

"It's okay," I said and laid my cheek against Jethro's dark brown neck. "What on earth happened?"

Jack pointed toward the railroad tracks that ran along the far side of the fence by the road. "You know how you told 'em not to set the first leg of the marathon so close to the train track?"

I nodded. "But thirty or forty trains have rattled by in the last two days. The horses couldn't have cared less. The show committee said I was crazy to worry."

"Uh-huh," Jack continued. I watched his enormous hands flex into fists. "The dumbass engineer on that last freight must-a decided it'd be cute to blow his whistle as long and loud as he could just when he got even with Jethro. Shoot, like to scared *me* half to death. No wonder Jethro spooked. If I ever find out that devil's name . . ."

Looking at Jack's face, I prayed for the engineer's sake that Jack never would find out his name. Jack was the kindest, gentlest man I knew until you messed with his horses. Then it was a thermo-nuclear explosion. I once saw him pick up an incompetent fill-in farrier at a horse show up by the scruff of his neck and toss him halfway down the barn aisle. The farrier had driven a nail straight into the quick of a mare's hoof, then went right on shoeing her after she thrashed and squealed. Frankly, I thought Jack had been extremely forbearing. I'd probably have cracked the man over the head with his hammer.

"Are the Hulls okay?" I asked. I'd been so busy worrying about Jethro, I hadn't given his drivers a thought.

"Tully's got a broken wrist and Amy's got a scraped chin. Other than maybe fifty thousand dollars worth of damage to vehicles and trailers, everybody's just fine, including Jethro. Thanks to you," Jack said.

Jethro still stood in the middle of my jacket, but there wasn't much point in moving him now. I doubted Pete Hull's insurance would include a new one. "I haven't run that hard since I was in high school." I leaned over and put my hands on my knees to steady my breathing. I'm well past thirty, although I don't generally let on just *how* well. I do have a daughter out of college, however, and though I'm in good shape, jogging in the park hadn't prepared me for running flat-out over a rutted hay field. It's a miracle I didn't trip, fall flat on my face and break my ankle. "Thank the Lord I didn't have to run any farther. Like to have killed me. Pure luck I caught him."

"And guts," Jack said and shook his head. "The insurance companies are going to have a field day on this one."

"Hey, girl, you're a hero!" Pete Hull trotted up and

smacked me on the shoulder.

"Just lucky, Pete. Y'all okay?"

"Gonna be. I told those idiots on the show committee we were asking for trouble to run the first leg of the marathon that close to the railroad track."

Still, it was easier to blame me, only a hired hand, after all, as the show manager, than to blame the show committee or the paying customers. Somehow I'd wind up carrying the can for the accident. Although it's a rule that drivers wear hard hats during the marathon, a number of the old guard still grumbled.

They all refused to wear hard hats during the other classes, although the rules say that no one can ever be penalized for choosing to wear one. The ladies preferred their summer straw hats festooned with feathers and ribbons. The men wanted their top hats and bowlers. Elegant, but those wouldn't protect their skulls in case of a runaway like Jethro's. The show committee would be after me to talk and talk and talk about whose fault Jethro's escapade was. If I hadn't needed my check, I would have run for my truck and ducked them. But I needed the money, even if I didn't get the accompanying smile and pat on the back for a job well done.

"Will you go with me to see the head of the show committee?" I asked Pete.

Before he could answer, my cell phone rang. I dragged it out of the pocket of my jeans and answered it, grateful for the interruption.

"Ms Abbott? Merideth Lackland Abbott?" an unfamiliar voice said. Male, heavy southern accent.

"Yes?"

"No easy way to say this, Mrs. Abbott. I'm afraid your father has met with an accident."

I grabbed Jack's arm. "Hiram? What happened? Is he all right?"

"Um, I'm sorry, but I'm afraid he's dead."

The next thing I knew I was sitting on the ground while Jack shoved my head down between my knees. That was when I threw up.

# Chapter 2

*Sunday Afternoon*
*Merry*

Pete Hull took the cell phone out of my hand and held it to his ear. "Give her a minute. Who is speaking, please?" I looked up at him as he listened, and I saw his face go slack. "Hiram? He's dead?" The buzz started at once among the people who were gathered around us. "How? . . . right." He listened some more, then handed the phone back to me. "Merry, honey, I'm so sorry."

I took the phone and stared at it as though it was a copperhead. Finally I put it to my ear. "This is Merideth Abbott again. Who did you say you were?" Must be a joke. Men like Hiram Lackland didn't just up and die.

"This is Sheriff Campbell of Bigelow County, Georgia."

"Oh, God, did he have an automobile accident? Was anybody else hurt?" Hiram had sworn he'd been sober for ten years, but Hiram had always been a good liar.

I stuck my finger in my ear to try to cut the noise around me and turned away from the crowd. I felt like an idiot still sitting on the grass, but I wasn't certain I could get up on my own. My father had been pushing seventy, but these days, that's practically middle-aged. There had to be some mistake. Hiram Lackland was indestructible. Lord knows he'd tried to kill himself often enough. He was like Jethro. He left a path of destruction behind him but always walked away sound.

"No, ma'am. Not an automobile accident."

"Don't tell me he turned over a carriage. He wasn't supposed to be driving alone."

"I'm afraid it was a freak accident. Look, Ms Abbott, it's kind of complicated to discuss over the phone. Where are you, exactly?"

Everyone except Pete had backed away. Jack was walking Jethro back to the barn. The others, I assumed, wanted to give me some privacy. Actually, I guess they really wanted to gossip about the whole Jethro incident. I reached up a hand so that Pete could pull me up. "I'm sitting on the ground in a pasture about fifty miles north of Chattanooga."

"You're not that far from Bigelow. We're in north Georgia."

"He emailed he was living in some little town called something-or-other Creek. What was he doing in Bigelow?"

"Um, Bigelow's the county seat. That's where the morgue is."

The morgue. That image hit me hard. Of course that's where they'd take him. He wouldn't care, but I did. I hunched my shoulders and said, "I can get on the road right now. How long is the drive to Bigelow?"

"Probably three hours or so. But, ma'am, he was living in Mossy Creek. That's where his place was."

"*Mossy* Creek. Now I remember. He said he had a studio apartment there in some woman's house."

"Yeah. Peggy Caldwell. She's the one who found him."

"*Found* him?

"She said you could stay with her as long as you need to. I'll call her and tell her to expect you tonight. You're going to be pretty worn out by the time you get here. It's not an easy drive. Not much Interstate. You got somebody with you? May not be a good idea you driving all this way alone right now."

"I'll be fine. I'm used to long-distance driving. But shouldn't I come to Bigelow instead? Do I have to identify I mean . . . "

"No, ma'am. Mrs. Caldwell already identified him. No reason you should have to go through that. Anyway, it's Sunday afternoon. Took us a while to track you down."

"I'm a horse show manager. I travel." I made scribbling motions with my hand. Pete scrounged a credit card receipt and pen out of his pockets.

"Ms. Abbott, nothin's going to change between now and tomorrow morning. You get you a good night's sleep and come in late morning. Bigelow's only about twenty minutes from Mossy Creek. We need to talk, and there's some paperwork we got to finish. And don't you worry. Mrs. Caldwell knows everybody. She can help you make whatever arrangements you need. I'll have somebody call her to tell her you'll be there this evening."

He gave me the number of the sheriff's department, and his private cell phone, which I thought was nice of him. Then he gave me Hiram's landlady's number and the address of Hiram's apartment in Mossy Creek, although Hiram had included it in his last email to me.

By the time I hung up, I felt utterly calm. That's the way I always handle disaster. It's what makes me a good show manager. After I solve the problem and calm everybody else down, that's when I go to pieces.

Even I couldn't solve this.

I started when I realized Pete still stood by with a look of concern on his face. "Oh, Pete, shouldn't you be with Tully and Amy?"

"They're in the EMT trailer getting patched up. Tully shooed me off to check on Jethro and you. I'm headed her way now. But Merry. Hiram. Dead? is Hiram really dead?"

"That's what the man said. Some kind of accident, but he didn't go into details."

"I can't believe it. I thought he'd outlive us all." He shook his head. "Irascible old bastard sorry, Merry."

I started to giggle, then clapped my hand over my mouth. If I started, I'd have hysterics. Once my mouth was shut, I felt tears ooze down my cheeks. "Good epitaph. He would have liked it." I squeezed Pete's shoulder. He winced. "Oh, I'm sorry."

"Bruises on my bruises. Probably won't be able to get out of bed in the morning. This whole thing is going to cost my insurance company a bundle." He took my arm and walked with me up toward the parking area. "I am seriously considering putting out a hit on the engineer runnin' that train. Damn fool."

Pete was rich and powerful enough to make life extremely

unpleasant for the man. "Don't you kill him, and whatever you do, don't tell Jack who he is or where to find him or he'll do the killin' for you. Tully would be angry if either one of you went to jail for manslaughter."

"Justifiable homicide." We stopped by my truck. "I'd hug you, but I'd probably scream in pain. You leaving now?"

"The show committee's bound to want to talk to me, but I can't deal with them right now."

"Don't you worry, I'll handle the show committee," Pete said. His face looked grim. He ran a multi-million dollar company. The show committee should be a piece of cake for him.

"And they owe me a check."

"You got a deposit slip in your purse? Give it to me. I'll pick up your check and deposit it tomorrow morning for you."

"Thanks Pete." I dug a deposit slip out of the satchel I use as a handbag and gave it to him. "I've already checked out of my motel. If they go on with the marathon, the show president can give out the awards anyway, so I was good to go right after the marathon until this happened."

"You get on the road. I'll do the explaining. "

I hesitated, half in and half out of the truck. "Pete, I didn't set that course close to the railroad track."

"Shoot, I know that. I won't let 'em use you as a scapegoat."

"If I leave now, it'll look like I'm running away," I said.

"Merry, your daddy just died! Git."

Jack walked up behind Pete. "Tully's hollering for you, Pete."

Pete nodded, patted my arm and limped toward the van the EMTs were using for their first aid station.

Jack stood at the door of my truck, waited for me to climb in and shut the door with a resounding smack. Mercifully, I had parked on the far side and away from Jethro's path of destruction, so my truck hadn't sustained even a denta *fresh* dent, at least. "Hiram was a fine horseman and a great trainer, Merry," Jack said. "Email us and let us know what's going on.

If you have a memorial service, I know some of us would like to come."

"Jack, it's to hell and gone in No-where, Georgia, but I'll let you know."

I could see him in my rear view mirror as I pulled out onto the road and turned toward the big wrought iron entrance gates of The Meadows, the farm that had hosted the show. As I drove over the railroad tracks to the road, I considered turning around. I did not want to face three hours of solitary driving with nothing to think about except the father I would never see again.

I made it as far as a Wal-Mart parking lot before I pulled over, stopped, put my head down on the steering wheel, and bawled. We were so close to reaching some sort of meeting of minds, my father and I. Now we'd never have the chance.

Eventually I gulped myself into silence. Then I got angry. "How dare you die on me, Hiram Lackland? I loved you. Now I can't tell you." I smacked the steering wheel so hard I yelped, took a deep breath and calmed down.

What was I supposed to do now? Any death involves protocols and rituals, Southern deaths more than most. Even In retirement Hiram Lackland was a large fish in the small pond of international carriage driving. A great many people would have to be notified.

I couldn't face all that this afternoon. Still, a couple of people had to know right now. I dialed my cell phone and listened to it ring. Just as I was about to hang up, this was not the sort of thing one left on voice mail, it was answered.

"Hello?" She sounded breathless. She'd probably been out in the garden. She usually was in the spring.

"Mom?"

"Merry? What's wrong? Oh, lordy, is it Allie?"

I hadn't heard the emotion in my voice, but she had and she'd jumped right to worrying about her granddaughter. "She's fine."

"You?"

"Not so good. Mom, Hiram's dead."

*Gayle Trent*

CPSIA information can be obtained at www.ICGtesting.com
Printed in the USA
241181LV00001B/23/P

9 780984 125845